D0988014

PATRICIA ST JOHN

Treasures of the Snow

Copyright © Patricia St John 1950
Second revised edition 2007, reprinted 2009

ISBN 978 1 84427 298 3

Scripture Union
207–209 Queensway, Bletchley, Milton Keynes, MK2 2EB, England
Email: info@scriptureunion.org.uk
Website: www.scriptureunion.org.uk

Scripture Union Australia
Locked Bag 2, Central Coast Business Centre, NSW 2252
Website: www.scriptureunion.org.au

Scripture Union USA
PO Box 987, Valley Forge, PA 19482
Website: www.scriptureunion.org

All rights reserved. No part of this publication may be reproduced, stored in a retrieval system, or transmitted in any form or by any means, electronic, mechanical, photocopying, recording or otherwise, without the prior permission of Scripture Union.

The right of Patricia St John to be identified as author of this work has been asserted by her in accordance with the Copyright, Designs and Patents Act 1988.

British Library Cataloguing-in-Publication Data.
A catalogue record of this book is available from the British Library.

Printed and bound in India by Thomson Press.

Internal illustrations by Gary Rees
Cover design by Go Ballistic
Internal design and layout by Author and Publisher Services

Scripture Union is an international Christian charity working with churches in more than 130 countries, providing resources to bring the good news about Jesus Christ to children, young people and families and to encourage them to develop spiritually through the Bible and prayer.

As well as our network of volunteers, staff and associates who run holidays, church-based events and school Christian groups, we produce a wide range of publications and support those who use our resources through training programmes.

Treasures of the Snow

A note from the author

When I was a child of 7, I went to live in Switzerland. My home was a chalet on the mountain, above the village where I have imagined Annette and Dani to live.

Like them, I went to the village school on a sledge by moonlight, and helped to make hay in summer. I followed the cows up the mountain, and slept in the hay. I went to church on Christmas Eve to see the tree covered with oranges and gingerbread bears. I was taken to visit the doctor in the town up the valley. Klaus was my own white kitten, given to me by a farmer, and my baby brothers rode in the milk cart behind the great St Bernard dog.

But all this was many years ago. Switzerland today is probably very different. I expect it would be impossible now for a child to miss school for any length of time, and no doubt the medical service has improved. Perhaps all little villages have their own doctors now.

But I do know that today, as all those years ago, the little school and the church still stand, the cowbells still tinkle in the valley, and the narcissi still scent the fields in May. And I hope that little children still sing carols under the tree at Christmas and love their gingerbread bears as much as I loved mine.

I have not given the village its proper name, because, for the sake of the story, I have added one or two things that are not really there. For instance, there is no town near that could not be reached except by the Pass. But otherwise I have tried to keep it true to life. If ever you go to Switzerland and take an electric train up from Montreux, you will stop at a tiny station where hay fields surround the platform, and high green hills rise up behind, dotted with chalets. To the right of the railway the banks drop down into a foaming, rushing river, beyond which the mountains rise again. Between a long green mountain and a rocky, pointed mountain there lies a Pass. If, added to all this, you see a low white school building not far from the station and a wooden church spire rising from behind a hillock, you will know that that is the village where this story was born.

1

It was Christmas Eve, and three figures were climbing the steep, white mountainside, the moonlight casting shadows behind them across the snow. The middle one was a woman in long petticoats and a dark cloak over her shoulders. Clinging to her hand was a black-haired boy of 6, who talked all the time with his mouth full. Walking apart, with her eyes turned to the stars, was a little girl of 7. Her hands were folded across her chest, and close against her heart she carried a golden gingerbread bear with eyes of white icing.

The little boy had also had a gingerbread bear, but he had eaten it all except the back legs. He looked at the little girl spitefully. "Mine was bigger than yours," he announced.

The girl seemed unconcerned. "I would not change," she replied calmly, without turning her head. Then she looked down again with eyes full of love at the beautiful creature in her arms. How solid he looked, how delicious he smelt, and how brightly he gleamed in the starlight. She would never eat him, never! Eighty little village children had been given gingerbread bears, but hers had surely been by far the most beautiful.

Yes, she would keep him for ever in memory of tonight. Whenever she looked at him she would remember Christmas Eve – the frosty blue sky, the warm glow of the lighted church, the tree decked with the silver stars, the carols, the crib, and the sweet, sad story of Christmas. It made her want to cry when she thought about the inn where there was no room. She would have opened her door wide and welcomed them in.

Lucien, the boy, was annoyed by her silence. "I have nearly finished mine," he remarked, scowling. "Let me taste yours, Annette. You have not begun it."

But Annette shook her head and held her bear a little closer. "I am never going to eat him," she replied. "I am going to keep him for ever and ever."

They had come to a parting of the ways. The crumbly white path lined with the sleigh tracks divided. A little way along the right fork stood a group of chalets with lights shining in their windows and dark barns massed behind them. Annette was nearly home.

Madame Morel hesitated. "Are you all right to run home alone, Annette?" she asked doubtfully, "or shall we take you to the door?"

"Oh, I would much rather go alone," answered Annette, "and thank you for taking me. Goodnight, Madame. Goodnight, Lucien."

She turned and fled, in case Madame should change her mind and insist on seeing her to the door, when she so badly wanted to be alone.

She wanted to get away from Lucien's chatter and wrap herself round with the silence of the night. How could she think, and look at the stars, when she was having to make polite replies to Madame Morel and Lucien?

She had never been out alone at night before, and even this was a sort of accident. She was to have gone to the church on the sleigh with Father and Mother; they had all been thinking about it and planning it for weeks. But that morning her mother had been taken ill and her father had gone off on the midday train to fetch the doctor from the town up the valley. The doctor had arrived about teatime, but he could not cure her in time to get up and go to church as Annette had hoped he would. So, to her great disappointment, she had had to go instead with Madame Morel from the chalet up the hill. But when she had reached the church it had been so beautiful that she had forgotten everything but the tree and the magic of Christmas, so it had not mattered so much after all.

The magic stayed with her. And now, as she stood alone among snow and stars, it seemed a pity to go in just yet. She hesitated as she reached the steps leading up to the balcony, and looked round. Just opposite loomed the cowshed; Annette could hear the animals moving and munching from the manger. A glorious idea struck her. She made up her mind in a moment, darted across the sleigh tracks and lifted the latch of the door. The warm smell of cattle and milk and hay greeted her as she slipped inside. She wriggled between the legs of the chestnut cow and wormed her way into the hayrack. The cow was having supper, but Annette flung her arms around her neck and let her go on munching. Surely the cows must have munched when Mary sat among them with her newborn baby in her arms, she thought to herself.

She looked down at the manger and imagined baby Jesus lying in the straw. Through a hole in the roof she could see one bright star. She remembered how a star had shone over Bethlehem and guided the wise men to the house where Jesus was. She could imagine them padding up the valley on their lurching camels. And surely any moment now the door would open softly, and the shepherds would come stealing in with little lambs in their arms. Perhaps they would offer to cover the child with woolly fleeces. As she leaned further over a great wave of pity swept over her for the homeless baby, against whom all doors had been shut.

"There would have been plenty of room in our chalet," she whispered, "and yet perhaps after all this is the nicest place. The hay is sweet and clean and Paquerette's breath is warm and pleasant. Maybe God chose the best cradle for his baby after all."

She might have stayed there dreaming all night had it not been for the gleam of a lantern through the half-open door of the shed, and the sound of firm, crunchy footsteps in the snow. Then she heard her father call her in a hurried, anxious voice.

She slipped down from the rack, dodged Paquerette's tail, and ran out to him with wide open arms.

"I went in to wish the cows a happy Christmas," she said, laughing. "Did you come out to find me?"

"Yes, I did," he replied, but he was not laughing. His face was pale and grave in the moonlight. He took her hand and almost dragged her up the steps. "You should have come in at once when your mother is so ill. She has been asking for you this last half hour."

Annette felt terrible about that. Somehow the Christmas tree had driven everything else out of her mind, and all the time her mother, whom she loved so much, was lying ill and wanting her. Annette had thought the doctor would have made her well. She took her hand from her father's and ran up the wooden stairs. She slipped into her mother's bedroom.

Neither the doctor nor the village nurse saw her until she had crept up to the bed, for she was a small, slim child who moved noiselessly as a shadow. But her mother saw her, and half held out her arms. Annette, without a word, ran into them and hid her face on her mother's shoulder. She began to cry quietly, for her mother's face was almost as white as the pillow and it frightened her. Besides, she felt sorry for having been away so long.

"Annette," whispered her mother, "stop crying; I have a present for you."

Annette stopped at once. A present? Of course, it was Christmas. She had quite forgotten. Her mother always gave her a present, but she usually had it on New Year's Day. Wherever could it be? She looked round expectantly.

Her mother turned to the nurse. "Give him to her," she whispered. And the nurse drew back the blanket and produced a bundle wrapped in a white shawl. She came round to Annette and held it out to her.

"Your little brother," the nurse explained. "Let us go down by the fire and you shall rock his cradle. We must leave your mother to sleep. Kiss her goodnight."

"Your little brother," echoed her mother's weak voice. "He is yours, Annette. Bring him up and love him and look after him for me. I give him to you."

Her voice trailed away and she closed her eyes. Annette, too dazed to speak, allowed herself to be led downstairs by the nurse. She sat down on a stool by the stove to rock the wooden cradle where her Christmas present lay smothered in shawls and blankets.

She sat very still for a long time, staring at her little brother. The snow cast a strange light on the walls, and the glow of the stove burned rosy on the ceiling. The house was very, very still, and the Christmas star shone in through the unshuttered windows. Annette remembered that a star had once shone on the other Christmas baby in Bethlehem. And she thought that Mary must have sat and watched God's little Son, just as she, Annette, was sitting by the stove watching her little brother.

She gently touched the top of his downy head, which was all she could see of him. Then with a tired sigh she leaned her head against the cradle and let her imagination roam where it would. Stars, shepherds, little new babies, shut doors, wise men and gingerbread bears... They all became muddled up in her mind, and she slid gradually on to the floor.

It was here that her father found her an hour later, lying as peacefully asleep as her baby brother, her bright head pillowed on the cradle rocker.

"Poor little motherless creatures," he said as he stooped to pick her up. "How shall I ever bring them up without her?"

For Annette's mother had gone to spend Christmas with the angels.

2

That was how Daniel Burnier, aged 3 hours, became the special property of Annette Burnier, aged 7 years.

The kind village nurse stayed for some time to bath and feed him. When she left, Annette's father paid a woman from the village to come and nurse him. But he belonged to Annette, and nobody ever spoke of him as anything but Annette's baby.

For, once the first great shock of her grief was over, Annette gathered up all the love of her sorrowful, lonely little heart and poured it out on her little brother. She held his bottle while he sucked, and sat quietly by his cradle in case he should wake and want her. It was Annette who ran to him in the night if he woke or whimpered. It was she who carried him out onto the balcony at midday so that the sun might shine on him. And in this atmosphere of love and sunshine the baby thrived. There was no other baby of his age in the valley to touch him for strength and beauty. He slept, and woke, and chuckled, and fed, and kicked, and slept again. In fact, he never gave a moment's anxiety to anyone.

"He was born under a lucky star," exclaimed the woman from the village, gazing at him thoughtfully.

"He was born under a Christmas star," said Annette solemnly. "I think he will always be good and happy."

And how he grew! By the time the sun was beginning to melt the snows, and the crocuses were pushing up in the pale fields, he was easily outgrowing his baby clothes. And as soon as the cows had gone up the mountain he cut his first tooth. As Annette knew nothing about first teeth, and expected no trouble, it seemed the baby himself forgot that it should have been a troublesome affair. So instead of fretting and crying, he merely giggled and sucked his fists.

By the time the beech leaves were flaming like golden torches among the dark pines and the first blizzards began to blow over the mountains, Dani was moving round, and his cradle could contain him no longer. He wanted to explore everything from the stove to the balcony steps. Annette spent an anxious few weeks hauling him out of danger. In the end she decided she could bear the strain no longer. So they tied him by one pink foot to the leg of the kitchen table, and he explored in circles. Life became more peaceful.

One evening, Annette, slipping down to the living room after tucking Dani up in his cradle, found her father sitting by the stove with his head in his hands. He looked old and tired and grey. He had often looked old and tired since his wife died, but tonight he looked worse than usual. Annette, who tried hard to make up for her mother, laid her soft cheek against his bony one.

"What is the matter, Papa?" she asked. "Are you very tired tonight? Shall I heat you a cup of coffee?"

He looked down at her curiously for a minute or two. She was so small and light, like some golden-haired fairy, but how sensible and womanly she was! Somehow during the past year he had made a habit of telling her his troubles. He had even listened to her serious advice. So now he drew her head against his shoulder and told her all about it. "We shall have to sell some of the cows, little daughter," he explained sadly. "We must have some more money or there will be no winter boots for you."

Annette raised her head and stared at him in horror. They had only ten cows, and each one was a personal friend. Any one of them would be missed terribly; she must think of a better way to earn money than that.

"You see," went on her father, "other men have wives to look after their little ones. I have to pay a woman to nurse Dani, and it doesn't come cheap. Yet someone must look after him, poor little boy."

Now Annette sat up very straight, and tossed back her plaits. She saw her way quite clearly. All she had to do was to make her father see it too.

"Papa," she said very slowly, "you do not need Mademoiselle Mottier any longer. I am 8½ now, and I can look after Dani as well as anyone. You will not have to pay me anything, and then we can keep the cows. Why, think, Papa, how unhappy they would be to leave us! I do believe Paquerette would cry!"

"But you must go to school," said her father rather doubtfully. "It would not be right to keep you at home. Anyhow, it is against the law. The master would want to know why, and he would tell the mayor and we should get into trouble."

"But it is much more important to look after Dani," answered Annette, wrinkling her forehead, "and if you explained to the master he would understand. He is kind, the master, and he is a friend of yours. Let us try it and see what happens. I will do my lessons here in the kitchen, Papa, every morning. Dani can play on the floor. And in any case, when he is 5 he will go to the infant school."

Her father continued to look at her thoughtfully. Small as she was, he thought she was as clever as a woman in looking after the baby. Also, he knew she was marvellously handy about the house. But she could not do the cooking, or knit the stockings, or do the rough heavy work. Besides, she ought to have some schooling. He sat thinking in silence for a full five minutes; then he had an idea.

"I wonder if your grandmother would come," he said suddenly. "She is old and has rheumatics, and her sight is poor. But she could do the cooking and mending, perhaps, and she could help you with your lessons in the evenings. It would be company for you, too, when I am up the mountain. You're too little a girl to be left alone all day long. If I write a letter to the master telling him that Grandmother will give you a bit of teaching, maybe he will agree to keep quiet about it."

Annette fetched two sheets of paper and the pen and ink from the cupboard.

"Write to them both now," she said, "and I will post the letters when I go for the bread. Then we shall get the answers nice and quickly."

Both letters were answered that week. The first answer was in the shape of Grandmother. She arrived by train, all bent over, with a wooden box roped up very securely. Annette went down to meet her, and watched the little electric train caterpillaring its way up the valley between the hay fields. It was late, the man at the wheel explained angrily, because a cow had strayed on to the line and the train had had to stop. He was so eager to move on quickly that Grandmother barely had time to get down from the train before it set off again. Her wooden box had to be hurled out after her while the train was moving.

Grandmother, however, seemed quite unmoved. She leaned on her stick and wanted to know how she was to get up the hill. Annette, who knew nothing about rheumatism, suggested that they should walk. Grandmother said, "Nonsense, child!" In the end, they got a lift in an empty farm cart that had brought cheeses down to the train and was now going back up the mountain. The road was stony, the wheels wooden, and the mule stumbled a lot. Annette enjoyed the ride very much more than Grandmother did. But the old woman gritted her teeth and made no complaint. She only let out a tired sigh of relief when she found herself safely on the sofa by the stove. She had a cushion at her aching back and Annette bustled about getting her some tea.

Dani came out from under the table, shuffling along on his backside. He stuck three fingers in his mouth and laughed at Grandmother. She put on her spectacles to see him better. They sat for some moments staring at each other, her dim old eyes meeting his forget-me-not blue ones. Then he threw back his head and laughed again.

"That child will wear out his trouser seat," said Grandmother, taking a piece of bread and butter and cherry jam. "He should be taught to crawl."

She said no more until she had finished her tea. Then she flicked the crumbs from her black skirt and rose, leaning heavily on her stick.

"So," she remarked, "I have come. What I can, I will do. What I cannot, you must do for me. Now, Annette, turn that baby the right way up and come and show me round the kitchen." From that moment Grandmother did what she could, Annette did the rest, and the household ran like clockwork. All except for Dani, who continued to move round and round the table leg on his seat in spite of Grandmother. So after a few days Annette was sent to the village to buy some thick black felt, and Grandmother sewed round patches onto the seats of all Dani's knickerbockers. He looked a little odd in them, but they served their purpose very well indeed. After all, they weren't seen much because they were nearly always underneath him.

The second answer arrived in the shape of the village schoolmaster. He came up from the valley late on Saturday afternoon to call on Monsieur Burnier. Annette's father was milking cows and saw him coming, out of the cowshed window. He did not want to argue with the schoolmaster because he was afraid of getting the worst of it. So he ran out of the back door and hid in the hay loft. Annette, who was also looking out of the living room window, saw her father's legs disappear up the ladder just as the schoolmaster came round the corner. She understood perfectly what was expected of her.

She opened the door and invited the master in, offering him most politely the best chair with a red plush seat. He was very fond of Annette, and Annette was very fond of him, but today they were a little bit shy of each other. Grandmother folded her hands and sat up straight. Her expression reminded Annette of a picture she had seen of an old warhorse scenting battle.

"Annette, I have come to see your father," began the schoolmaster, coughing nervously, "to discuss his letter about your being absent from school. I cannot say that I think it right for a little girl of your age. Besides, it is against the law of the State."

"The State will know nothing about Annette unless you choose to mention her," said Grandmother shortly. "Besides, I will educate the child myself. I do not think it right for a little boy of Daniel's age to be left without his sister to look after him."

"But can't you look after him?" suggested the schoolmaster gently.

"Certainly not," snapped Grandmother, "my sight is so poor that I cannot see where he is going. My arms are so rheumaticky that I cannot pick him up if he falls. Besides, he moves like an express train, and I am nearly 80. You do not know what you are talking about."

The schoolmaster gazed at Dani, who was playing on the floor. There was nothing much to be seen of him but the black felt patch and his dimpled legs.

The schoolmaster frowned.

"When will your father be in, Annette?" he asked.

"I do not know. He may not be back for some time. It is not worth your while to wait, monsieur," replied Annette steadily. She knew perfectly well that her father would return just as soon as the master's hat disappeared down the valley.

The schoolmaster sat thinking. He was a good man, and really cared about Annette and his duty towards her. Yet he did not want to give up her father, his old friend, into the hands of the law. He could see that the child was needed at home. At last he had an idea. He did not think that it was a very good one, but it was better than nothing. He turned to Grandmother.

"I will let the matter rest on one condition only. That is, that every Saturday morning when Annette comes down for the bread, she shall visit me in my house. I will give her some tests to see if she is making progress in her studies at home. I will say no more. But if I find she is learning nothing then I shall feel it my duty to insist that she attends school like other children."

He tried to speak sternly, but Annette beamed at him. Dani, sensing a family victory, suddenly turned himself the right way up and laughed. The schoolmaster looked at the two fair, motherless children for a moment, smiled and took his leave. As soon as he had disappeared into the pinewood, Annette ran to the door and called to her father to come down from the hay loft.

So every Saturday morning Annette rapped at the front door of the tall white house where the schoolmaster lived, with her breadbasket on her back and her tattered exercise book in her hand. In the winter they sat by the stove and ate spiced fruit tart made by the schoolmaster's friendly housekeeper, and drank hot chocolate. In the summer they sat on the veranda and ate cherries and drank apple juice. After that the tests would begin.

They always started with arithmetic, but Annette was no good at arithmetic, and struggled with her answers. After a few minutes, they would pass on to history. The schoolmaster did not have to set test questions for this subject, for Annette loved history. She would lean forward, clasping her knees, and talk about how William Tell had won the freedom of Switzerland. She would tell the story of how his brave little son had stood still while an apple had been placed on his head and was split by his father's whizzing arrow. She would tell of the brave prisoner of the lakeside castle of Chillon, who paced his cell until the very paving stones were worn by his footsteps. She would tell of the division of Switzerland into regions called Cantons.

And then she would tell how the beautiful Luce had gone out to drive her cows to pasture and had been carried off by the lord of Gruyère Castle. She had pined away in her stone prison, yearning for the forests and the fields and the Alpine slopes, and had died of a broken heart. Annette's voice almost shook when she spoke of the beautiful captive.

Then they would go over the stories of the Waldensian martyrs, who were persecuted for their religion, and who went to their death singing praises. Their bodies were hurled over the precipices, but their faith and love lived on and their spirits went happily to God. Annette and the schoolmaster would look at each other with shining eyes, for they both loved courage. And after this they would turn to the Bible which Annette was beginning to know quite well, for she read it aloud to Grandmother every evening.

By this time the schoolmaster would have forgotten to tell Annette off because she wasn't very good at arithmetic. Instead he would give her fresh books to read, and the housekeeper would fill the gaps in her breadbasket with spiced gingerbread hearts and knobbly chocolate sticks wrapped in silver paper. Then Annette would say goodbye. The schoolmaster and his housekeeper would stand at the door and watch her until she reached the edge of the pinewood. Here, she always turned round to wave.

"What a dear little girl," the housekeeper would say.

"Yes," the schoolmaster would reply, with a sigh. "If only she would learn her arithmetic!"

3

It was Christmas Eve again, five years after the beginning of this story. Dani was therefore 5 years old. It was a great day, because for the first time in his life he had been considered old enough to go down to the church with Annette to see the tree.

Now he sat up in bed, eating a bowl of potato soup. His yellow head only just showed above his enormous white feather duvet, which was almost as fat as it was broad. Annette sat beside him, and in her hand she held a shining gingerbread bear.

"I am sorry, Dani," she announced firmly, "but you cannot have the bear in the bed with you. It would be all crumbs by the morning. Look! I will put him here on the cupboard. The moon will shine in on him and you will be able to see him."

Dani opened his mouth to argue, but changed his mind, and filled his mouth with potato soup. It was unreasonable of his sister to object to his hugging his bear all night. But, after all, there were lots of other things to be happy about. Dani was always happy, from the moment when he opened his eyes in the morning to the moment he closed them at night. Tonight he was especially happy because he had heard the bells and seen the glittering tree, and been out in the snow by starlight. He handed his empty bowl to Annette and cuddled down under his feather duvet.

"Do you think," he asked, "that Father Christmas would come if I put my slippers on the windowsill?"

Annette was rather startled. She wondered where he had heard of such a thing. (In Switzerland at that time, Father Christmas was not such a well known person as in other countries. Swiss children had their Christmas bear from the tree on Christmas Eve, and presents from their family on New Year's Day. On Christmas Day they went to church and had a feast, but few children got a present.)

"I heard," went on Dani, "that he came on a sleigh drawn by reindeer, and left presents in good children's slippers. Am I a good child, Annette?"

"Yes," answered Annette, kissing him, "you are a very good child, but you will not get a present from Father Christmas. He only goes to rich little boys."

"Aren't I a rich little boy?" asked Dani, who thought he had everything he wanted in life.

"No, Dani," replied Annette firmly, "you are not rich. We are poor and Papa has to work hard. Grandma and I have to go on and on patching your clothes because we cannot afford to buy new ones."

Dani chuckled. "I don't mind being poor. I like it. Now tell me a story, Annette. Tell me about Christmas and the little baby and the cows and the great big shining star."

So Annette told the story, and Dani, who should have been asleep, listened wide-eyed.

"I should have liked sleeping in the hay better than in the inn," he said when she had finished. "I should like to sleep with Paquerette. I think it would be fun."

Annette shook her head. "No, you wouldn't like it at all," she replied."Not in the winter without a duvet. You would be very cold and unhappy and long for a warm bed. It was cruel of them to say there was no room for a little new baby. They could have made room somehow."

The cuckoo clock on the stairs struck nine. Annette jumped up.

"You must go to sleep, Dani," she said, "and I must make Papa's hot chocolate."

She kissed her brother, tucked him up, put out the light and left him. But Dani did not go to sleep. Instead, he lay staring out into the darkness, thinking hard.

He was not a greedy little boy, but he could not help thinking that if Father Christmas happened to come to their house it would be a great pity not to be ready. Of course, it was unlikely he would come, since Dani was only a poor child. But on the other hand, it was just possible that he might. And, after all, it could do no harm to put out the little slipper even if there were nothing in it in the morning. The question was where to put it. He could not put it on the windowsill, because he could not open the high barred shutters by himself. Nor could he put it outside the front door, because the family were all sitting in the living room. The only place was just outside the back door on the little strip of snow that divided the kitchen from the hay barn. Of course, Father Christmas was very unlikely to see it there. But still, there was no harm in trying.

Dani's mind was made up. He crept out of bed and tiptoed cautiously across the bedroom and down the stairs. He went barefoot, because he did not want anyone to hear him. In his hand he carried one small, scarlet, fur-lined slipper. Annette had made it, and Dani felt it might catch the eye of Father Christmas. It was a struggle to lift the great wooden bar that latched the kitchen door. Dani had to stand on a stool before he managed it. He had a moment's bright vision of snow and starlight, and then the bitter air struck him and almost took his breath away. He thrust the slipper onto the step, and shut the door again as quickly as he could.

Back to bed scuttled Dani with a light heart. He cuddled down under the clothes, curled himself into a ball, and buried his nose in the pillows. He had already said his proper prayers with Annette before he got into bed, but now he had a little bit to add.

"Please, dear God," he whispered, "make Father Christmas and his reindeer come this way. And make him see my scarlet slipper. Make him put a little present inside, even if I am only a poor little boy."

And then Dani rolled over sideways. He fell asleep to dream, like thousands of other children the world over, of the old Gentleman in the red cloak careering over the snow to the jangle of reindeer bells.

He woke very early, and of course the first thing he thought of was the scarlet slipper. It was such an exciting thought that his heart started to thump. He peeped over the top of his duvet to see whether Annette was awake.

But Annette was fast asleep, with her long fair hair spread all over the pillow. For all Dani knew, it might have been the middle of the night. In fact, he had almost decided that it must still be the middle of the night, when he heard his father clattering the milk churns in the kitchen below.

So it must be Christmas morning! Dani must get down quickly or his father would open the door and find his present before he did. Somehow, Dani was absolutely sure that there would be a present. All his doubts of the night before had vanished in his sleep.

He crept out of the room without waking Annette. He slipped into the kitchen where his father was scalding the churns. His father did not see him until he felt two arms clasping his legs, and looked down. There was his son, rosy, bright-eyed and tousled, looking up at him.

"Has Father Christmas been?" asked Dani. Surely his father, who stayed up so late, and got up so early, must have heard the bells and the crunch of hooves in the snow.

"Father Christmas?" repeated his father in bewilderment. Then he smiled. "Why, no, he didn't come here. We live too far up the mountain for him."

But Dani shook his head. "We don't," he said eagerly. "His reindeers can go anywhere. I expect you were asleep and didn't hear him. Open the door for me, Papa, just in case he has left me a present."

His father wished he had known of this earlier, so that he could have put a chocolate stick on the step, for he hated to see the boy disappointed. However, open the back door he must, to roll the churns across to the stable. So he lifted the latch, and in an instant Dani had dived between his legs like an eager rabbit, and was kneeling by his slipper in the snow.

Then he gave a wild, high-pitched scream of excitement and dived back again into the kitchen with his slipper in his arms.

A miracle had happened: Father Christmas had been, and had left a present! In all his happy five years of life, Dani had never had such a perfect present before.

For curled up in the furry lining of his scarlet slipper was a tiny white kitten, with blue eyes and one black smudge on her nose. It was a weak, thin little kitten, very nearly dead with cold and hunger. Had it not been for the warmth of the fur lining it would certainly have been quite dead. But it still breathed lightly. Dani's father, forgetting all about the churns, knelt down on the kitchen floor beside his son and set about helping the kitten.

First he wrapped it in a piece of hot flannel and laid it against the hot wall of the stove. Then he heated milk in a pan and fed it with a spoon, as it was far too weak to suck. At first it only spluttered and dribbled. But after a while it put out a tiny pink tongue and its dim blue eyes grew bright and interested. Then, after about five minutes or so, it twitched its tail and stretched itself. Finally, having had quite enough to eat, it curled itself back into a ball and set up a faint, contented purr.

All this time Dani and his father had not spoken one word, because they were so busy helping the kitten. But, now that their work was successfully finished for the time being, they sat back and looked at each other. Dani's cheeks were the colour of poppies and his eyes shone like stars.

"I knew he would come," he whispered, "but I never guessed he would bring such a beautiful present. It's the most beautiful present I have ever had in all my life. What shall I call it, Papa?"

"You had better call it Klaus after the Christmas saint," said Papa. And he looked curiously at Dani with a sort of new respect. It certainly seemed like a miracle.

He left the sleeping kitten in Dani's care and went to the stables. Sitting in the dim light with his head pressed against the flanks of the cows, and the milk frothing into the pails, he tried to think of some explanation. Of course the kitten had strayed across from the barn. But it did seem wonderful that it should have found Dani's slipper and been there all ready for him. After a while, Dani's father decided that perhaps it was not so wonderful after all. Surely it was natural on Christmas Eve that the Father in heaven, thinking of his own Son, would not have wanted to disappoint a motherless child on earth. Surely he had guided the steps of the white kitten for the sake of Jesus, the baby born in Bethlehem. Dani's father paused for a moment in his milking and thanked God on behalf of his little son.

Annette appeared in the kitchen shortly afterwards to get breakfast. She stood still in amazement at the sight of Dani in his nightshirt and overcoat watching over a white kitten. She was about to ask questions when Dani put his finger on his lip and said, "Shh!" Then he tiptoed over to her, pulled her down on a chair, climbed onto her knee and whispered the whole strange story into her ear.

Annette had no difficulty in explaining it to herself. She believed that such a pure white kitten must have dropped straight from heaven. She sat down on the floor and gathered Dani and the kitten onto her lap. Here Grandmother found them half an hour later, when she came in expecting to find her Christmas coffee steaming on the table.

4

Lucien lay under his large feather duvet and wished it was not time to get up. His bed was so warm, and the air outside so cold. He sighed and cuddled down again.

"Lucien!" His mother's voice sounded really angry, and Lucien jumped up in a hurry. This was the third time she had called him, and before he had pretended not to hear. He could still get up and be in time for school, although he would not have time to do the milking. But if he didn't do the milking his mother would have to, and these days she did it more often than not.

"Other boys don't have to milk before they go to school," muttered Lucien, as he buttoned his jacket, "and I don't see why I should always have to work harder than everyone else just because I don't happen to have a father."

He went downstairs looking sulky and defiant. He sat down to gobble up his bread and coffee. His mother came in from the stable when he was halfway through.

"Lucien," she said sharply, "why don't you get up when I call you? It happens day after day! You're no help to me in the mornings at all. Your sister gets up early enough and goes off to work without any fuss. I know other boys have fathers, but we've only got three cows and we can't live without them. You're a big, strong boy now, and it's shameful that you should leave all the early work to me like this."

Lucien scowled. "I work at night," he whined. "I never get any play. I have to fetch in the wood, and I have to come further up the hill than any of the others. I fetch down the fodder for you, and clean the shed on Saturdays."

His mother sniffed. "I've usually done most of it by the time you get home from school," she retorted. "I know you don't get as much time in the winter as other children. But I do all I can, and this early morning milking is wearing me out. You're quite old enough to do it, and in future you're to get up properly. Now hurry off or you'll be late for school."

Lucien struggled into his cloak, and turned away with a sulky goodbye. He unhitched his sledge and went whizzing away into the frosty dark. Save for the smooth sound of his own runners, the world was silent with that tremendous silence that holds its breath before the coming of dawn. The enormousness of it usually awed Lucien a little, but today he was too cross to think about it.

"It's so unfair!" he muttered. "Everyone's against me – it's not my fault I don't get my lessons done properly. I'm always having to work at home. It's reading today. I suppose I shall be bottom of the class again, and that show-off Annette Burnier will be top. I bet she doesn't have to milk the cows before school… OH… !!"

He tried to stop, but it was too late. He had reached the fork in the path, and he had been so busy feeling cross that he had not looked where he was going. He had bumped straight into Annette's sledge sideways, and lifted her clean into the ditch.

It was a careless thing to do, and Lucien, crimson in the face and truly upset, jumped off his sledge to help. But Annette, who had never liked Lucien much, turned on him, waist deep in snow, her eyes blazing.

"You stupid boy!" she shouted, half crying. "Can't you look where you're going? Look at my exercise book – all my work is smudged and torn! I shall tell the master it's all your fault."

Lucien, who was never good at keeping his temper, lost it at once.

"All right!" he shouted back. "There's no need to make such a fuss. I didn't do it on purpose. Anyone would think I'd killed you instead of tearing your old exercise book. It won't hurt you to lose your marks. I'm going on."

He jumped onto his sledge and whizzed away, arriving just in time for school. Inside he felt really bad about it, but his manners were never very good at the best of times, and now he tried not to think of what he had done.

"She's only got to get out of that ditch," he muttered, "and I don't suppose she would have let me help her in any case. Thank goodness I'm in time for school. I've been late twice this week already."

But getting out of that snowdrift was a very different matter from getting in, and poor Annette had quite a struggle. By the time she had managed to get herself out and collect her books, she was crying hard. She was crying with cold and shock and because her knees were sore. But most of all, she was crying with rage. And when she crept into school a quarter of an hour later, her eyes were red and her nose was blue. Her raw hands and knees were grazed and bleeding. She certainly looked a sorry sight.

"Annette!" said the master, concerned. "What has happened to you?"

For a few seconds Annette fought hard with the temptation to tell tales. But the sight of Lucien sitting so smug and safe in his desk was too much for her.

"It was Lucien," she burst out angrily. "He knocked me into a ditch, and went off and left me. I couldn't get out." She stuffed her knuckles into her eyes and began crying again. She was really very badly shaken, and oh, so angry!

The class began to mutter and whisper. Lucien hung his head, and looked very sullen indeed.

The master dealt with Lucien most severely. He made the boy feel very small indeed, and seeing that, Annette cheered up and felt better. Then later the marks were read out, and Annette came top and felt better still. Lucien came bottom and was told to stay in and do extra work after school. So he sat through morning classes, had his dinner, came back to afternoon school, and then sat alone when the others had gone. And all the time the rage and hatred and ill-temper in his heart were getting bigger and bigger till he felt as if he were going to burst.

At last he was free. He wandered up the hill dragging his sledge behind him. What a terrible day it had been! His mother had been cross with him, Annette had told tales about him, the master had made him feel small, and he had come bottom of the class.

The shadows on the fields were strangely blue that night – a sort of unearthly blue, like the blue of mists in far valleys, or the blue of a wood pigeon's breast. High up, the mountaintops were still sunlit, with ragged wisps of cloud trailing about them. The quietness of the mountains seemed to hold out its arms to Lucien and he began to feel slightly comforted. So, as he trudged up the hill, Lucien's rage began to give place to a sort of weary misery, and, thinking he was alone, he began to cry a little.

Then he suddenly discovered that he was not alone. He was again at the place where the path divided. A little boy was standing in the snow looking up at him in great astonishment. He was a happy, rosy-cheeked, bright-eyed little boy, his fair hair sticking out like a thatch from under his woolly cap, his face glowing with good health and good humour.

It was Dani, making a snowman. He had just put on the head, and was arranging the eyes. It was the best snowman Dani had ever made, and he was just about to fetch Annette to look at it.

"Why are you crying?" asked Dani.

"I'm not crying!" retorted Lucien, angrily.

"Ooh, you are!" replied Dani, "and I know why... it's because the master shouted at you. Annette told me."

He did not mean to be cruel, for he was usually a kind little boy. But Lucien had been nasty to Annette and that, to Dani, was really bad. Lucien's temper flared up instantly, and lifting his foot, he kicked Dani's snowman into little bits. Dani screamed in alarm and disappointment.

Annette, crossing from the shed, saw what was happening in an instant. She flew down the path like a young tigress, and pushed Lucien hard. Lucien was about to push her back, but the sight of Monsieur Burnier coming out of the chalet with a bucket made him think better of it. He thought everything was clearly against him.

"Sneak – telltale – coward!" shouted Lucien. "Baby! coming into school crying like that."

"You great bully!" shouted back Annette, "leaving me in the ditch like that, and then kicking poor Dani's snowman! He never did you any harm. Why can't you leave him alone? I'm glad the master made you look stupid. Come on, Dani, come home."

She marched angrily off up the path, with Dani trotting behind her. But at the door of the chalet she turned and noticed a patch of pink sky behind the far mountains. Once, Grandmother had told her that the Bible said "Don't go to bed angry". Well, there was still time to apologise.

Lucien was still there. After all, it was nasty of her to have told tales. She hesitated.

But no – he'd been much worse than she had. It was for *him* to say he was sorry. If she asked him to forgive her it would sound as if she were to blame, and of course she wasn't – oh, no, not in the least! She went in and slammed the door behind her.

Lucien went slowly home, more furious than he had been all day long. But, as he walked, he glanced up and noticed a wonderful thing. The clouds had come up in a purple bank, blotting out the mountain behind his home. But just in one spot they had broken, and in that rift Lucien could see the snowy crest, radiant with golden light. It was like the rampart of some amazing city, bathed with the glory of God, seen through a veil, for a moment only.

Used as he was to winter sunsets, the beauty of this made Lucien catch his breath and look again. And the pure, high radiance suddenly made his anger seem a small, poor thing, not worth hanging on to. How nice it would be to start again! He could just go and say sorry to Annette…

But no! Annette was stuck-up, and would probably take no notice of him. And, anyhow, why should he apologise to that horrible girl?

So, because neither would be the first to forgive, the quarrel began. A quarrel that was to last a long time and was to bring a great deal of unhappiness for them both.

And as Lucien stood there thinking, a cloud blew across the break, and the amazing city was hidden from view.

5

Annette's birthday was in March. Dani made lots of plans for it, as nothing pleased Dani so much as giving presents. Some people might have said that his presents were not worth a great deal, but Dani thought they were beautiful. He kept them in a secret cupboard meant for storing wood. Annette knew that she must never go there, and pretended to think that it was full of wood chips for the stove.

Already the cupboard contained a family of fir cones, painted all different colours and arranged in a row. Father fir cone was red, Mother fir cone was green, and there were five little fir cones painted bright yellow. Then there was a beautiful picture Dani had drawn of Paquerette, the fawn cow, grazing in a field of enormous blue gentians nearly as big as herself. There was a pure white pebble, and a little bracelet made from the plaited hairs of the bull's tail. Sometimes there was a chocolate stick, but it never stayed long. Dani loved chocolate sticks and usually ate it himself after a day or two.

But now the great day was drawing very near, and tomorrow would be the real birthday. Dani's head was full of it, and as soon as Annette had gone to school, Dani explained his plan to Grandmother. She was sitting on the veranda in the spring sunshine chopping dandelion leaves for that evening's soup when her little grandson came up and rested his elbows on her knee.

"Grandma," announced Dani. "I'm going up the mountain to where the snow has melted, to pick soldanellas and crocuses for Annette's birthday. I will put them on the breakfast table with all my presents."

His grandmother, who hated his being out of her sight, looked doubtful.

"You are too little to go up the mountain alone," she replied. "The slopes are slippery and you will fall into the snowdrifts."

"Klaus will go with me," said Dani.

Grandmother chuckled. "A lot of good may she do you," she retorted. Then she gave a little shriek because Klaus, without the slightest warning, had leaped into Grandmother's lap. Klaus began rubbing her white head against the old woman, purring lovingly.

"Klaus knew we were talking about her," Dani smiled. "She knows everything, and she is just telling you that she will look after me up the mountain."

He picked his kitten up round the middle, kissed Grandmother, and stumped off down the balcony steps, singing a happy little song about the grand ladies who danced on the bridge at Avignon. Crash! crash! went his hobnailed boots, and his voice rose loud and clear. His grandmother strained her dim old eyes to watch him until out of sight, then she gave a little sigh and went on with her dandelions. He was growing so big and independent, and in a very short time he must start at the infant school. He was a baby no longer.

Dani trotted on up the slopes, and Klaus picked her way delicately behind him, for although she was a Christmas kitten she hated walking in the snow. It was a beautiful day, and spring was clothing the mountains and melting the drifts. Already the fields were green beside the river in the valley, and the cows were grazing out of doors. Up here on the higher slopes the snow was beginning to disappear, and there were patches of pale yellow grass, while the streams were swollen to overflowing with clear green ice water.

Klaus continued to pick her way until she reached the low stone wall at the edge of the field. On the other side of this stone wall was a rocky ravine with a rushing torrent at the bottom. In summer the rocks were like fairy gardens, with harebells and saxifrage and cushions of pink soapwort growing all over them. But now they were bare and brown. Klaus sat on the wall and fluffed out her fur in the spring sunshine. Then she started to wash herself all over, which was unnecessary because she was already almost as white as the snow.

Dani wandered from yellow patch to yellow patch, gathering flowers. The field was alive with pale mauve crocuses and bright primulas that followed the windings of the streams in the grass like little pink paths. Dani loved them, but what he loved best of all were the soldanellas. They could not even wait for the snow to melt, but pushed right up through the frozen edges of the drifts, their frail stems encased in ice. Their flowers, like fringed mauve bells, hung downwards.

Dani loved all beautiful things, and in this field of flowers he was as happy as a child could be. The sun shone on him and the flowers smiled up at him. Dani told himself stories about tiny goblins that lived in caves under the snow. Their beards were white and their caps were red and they were full of mischief. Sometimes, if there was no one looking, they came out and swung on the soldanella bells – Annette had said so.

For this reason he approached each fresh soldanella clump on tiptoe, and kept his eyes fixed on their bowed heads. And that was why he never heard footsteps approaching until they were quite close. Then he looked up suddenly with a little start.

Lucien stood close behind him, with a really unpleasant look on his face, and a gleam of triumph in his eyes. He had not forgotten the push that Annette had given him when Dani had screamed for help. Ever since that day he had planned some revenge, and when he had seen Dani's little figure standing alone in the high pasture he had hurried to the spot. He told himself he would not hurt such a tiny child, but it would be fun to tease and annoy him. At least he could take his flowers from him.

"Who are you picking those for?" demanded Lucien.

"For Annette," replied Dani. He had a feeling that Lucien would not like this answer, but Annette had told him that he must always speak the truth, even when he was frightened.

Lucien gave a nasty laugh.

"Annette! She's so stuck-up. But she's stupid, really, even though she pretends to be clever. The little ones in the infant school are better at sums than she is. She knows no more than her own cows. Give those flowers to me. Why waste them on her? I *hate* Annette."

Dani was so shocked at this speech that he went bright red, and put his flowers behind his back. How could anyone hate Annette? Annette who was so beautiful and so good, and so clever and so wise? Dani, who had never heard of jealousy, could not understand it.

"You can't have them," said Dani, holding the bunch tightly in his small hands. "They're mine."

"I shall take them," replied Lucien. "You can't fight against me, you baby! I can do what I like to you. And I shall."

He snatched the bunch roughly from Dani's grasp and flung them on the ground and trampled on them. Dani stared for a moment at the crushed soldanellas and bruised crocuses, and then burst into a loud howl. He had spent the whole happy afternoon gathering those flowers, and now they were all wasted. Then he flung himself on Lucien and began beating him with his small fists.

"I shall tell my papa," he shouted. "I shall go straight home and tell him this very minute and he will come to your house and you'll be in trouble!"

Now this was exactly what Lucien did not wish to happen, for, like most bullies, he was cowardly. He was really afraid of Dani's father. Dani's father was as tall and strong as a giant, and any ill-treatment of his son would certainly make him furious. Lucien held Dani firmly by the wrists to stop him punching, and looked round the field, wondering what he could do to frighten the little boy into silence.

His gaze suddenly fell on Klaus sunning herself on the wall, and an idea struck him. He pushed Dani away and walked rapidly towards the ravine. Dani, who thought his tormentor had left him, wiped away his tears with the back of his hand and began picking fresh flowers as fast as he could. Lucien or no Lucien, Annette's birthday table must be beautiful.

Suddenly Lucien's voice came ringing across the field. Dani looked up quickly, and what he saw made him feel quite sick for a moment. Lucien was standing by the wall holding Klaus out at arm's length by the scruff of her neck. He was holding her right over the dark ravine and the rushing torrent of melted ice.

"Unless you come here at once, and promise not to tell tales to your father," called Lucien, "I shall drop your kitten into the river."

Dani began to run, stumbling blindly over the snowdrifts, but his legs were trembling and he could not run fast. The thought of Klaus carried away helpless in that swirling brown current filled him with such horror that his mouth went dry and he could not cry out. He only knew that he must get there and snatch his kitten out of the grasp of that terrible boy and never, ever let Klaus go again.

Now, Lucien never for one moment meant to drop Klaus. He was a bully, but he wouldn't hurt a kitten. But Klaus was not used to being held by the scruff of the neck, and after a moment or two she began to struggle. Finally, getting frantic, she did what she had never done before. She put up her front paw and gave Lucien a sharp scratch.

Lucien, who was watching Dani stumble towards him, was taken by surprise and let go. Klaus dropped like a stone into the ravine, just as Dani, white and tearful, reached the wall.

Dani did not hesitate a single moment. He gave a shriek like some small, terrified animal caught in a trap, and hurled himself over the low wall. Lucien was quite paralysed for a few seconds by what he had done. He did not have time to grab Dani and pull him back.

After that everything happened in a few seconds. Klaus had not fallen into the water. She had stuck fast on a ledge of overhanging rock and clung there mewing piteously. An older child might have reached her safely and scrambled back, but Dani was only 5. The face of the rock was wet and Dani's feet slipped just as he reached his kitten. He gave another scream – a scream that haunted Lucien for years to come – and disappeared over the edge.

Had Lucien not been half stupid with panic he would have scrambled down after Dani and peered over into the ravine. But he never thought that Dani could be anything but dead. To see the body of the child carried away by the current, down towards the waterfall, was more than he could bear. He sank down on the grass in a limp little heap and covered his face with his arm.

"Dani's drowned!" he moaned over and over again. "I've killed him! What shall I do? Oh, what shall I do?"

But gradually a cowardly idea came into his mind, and he sprang up and looked round wildly. Time was getting on. They would soon come and look for Dani, and then they would find him and everyone would know that he was a murderer. No one so far knew that he had had anything to do with the accident. If he hurried home and behaved as if nothing had happened, no one ever would know. He must escape.

He ran like a hunted rabbit into the shelter of the pinewood, with his heart beating furiously and his head throbbing. He made his way home by lonely paths, so that if anyone should see him coming it would look as though he had come from another direction. Every few minutes he thought he heard footsteps following and leaped round to look. But there was no one there.

At last he reached his own back door, and here he stopped. No, he could not go in. He could not face his mother, who believed in him, with that dreadful secret in his heart. Surely she would see it in his face. He could not look the same as before. He was a murderer. Perhaps later he would summon up the courage to face her. But not yet, for his teeth were chattering so, and she would ask what was the matter. In the meantime, he must hide. He looked round wildly for some place, and saw the ladder leaning against the barn where the straw was stored in the attic above the cowshed. Up the ladder went Lucien, and then, flinging himself face downward in the chaff, he sobbed as though his heart would break.

6

The old grandmother finished shredding the dandelions and then, leaning heavily on her stick, went back into the house and sat down on her chair. She was very tired, and soon her head began to nod and she fell asleep.

Grandmother could hardly walk at all now and was nearly blind. She was usually very, very tired. But she loved her two grandchildren very much and was going to work for them till she dropped. So she continued to cook with swollen, hurting hands and to mend with strained, aching eyes. Annette never knew, for she was only 12 and Grandmother never complained.

Grandmother slept much longer than usual. Annette had gone down to the village to shop, and Father was up in the forest, cutting and stacking logs. Grandmother had meant to mend Dani's white woollen stockings, and put patches on the elbows of his blue linen overalls. But she was much too tired. She just folded her knotted old hands on her lap and went on sleeping. The cuckoo jumped out of the clock and struck three without waking her.

It was nearly four when Grandmother woke and looked at the clock, and then she gave a little exclamation of anxiety and surprise. Dani had gone out at half-past two and had not yet returned. Where could he be?

"Dani!" she called out sharply, for he might be hiding. Perhaps in a moment he would tumble out of the cupboard, mischievous and giggling.

But there was no answer, and Grandmother hobbled onto the veranda and shaded her dim eyes. Perhaps she would catch sight of him stumping home. How she would scold him for being so late!

A figure appeared round the cowshed, but it was not Dani. It was Annette with her basket on her back and a long golden loaf sticking out of the top of it. She had had a half holiday and had been shopping. She waved to Grandmother and came running up the steps.

"Annette," said Grandmother, "take your basket off and go and search for your little brother. He went out to pick flowers nearly an hour and a half ago and he hasn't come back."

Annette let down her basket with a bump. She thought that her grandmother was rather fussy about Dani. What harm could come to him, wandering about in fields where anyone he might meet knew him and loved him?

"He will be up in the woods with Papa," she replied. "I'll go up and see in a few minutes. Let me have a piece of bread and jam first, Grandma. I'm hungry."

She broke off a thick hunk from the loaf, and spread it with butter and jam, while her grandmother went back to the balcony and peered up the path again. Then while Annette was eating, firm footsteps were heard down the hillside and Father came into sight.

"Where is Dani?" cried Grandmother. "Has he not been with you, Michel? Did you not meet him up the mountain?"

"Dani?" repeated Father in astonishment. "He has not been near me. When did he leave you, Mother?"

Grandmother gave up trying to hide her anxiety and wrung her hands. "He left me over an hour and a half ago," she cried. "He and the kitten. He went out to pick crocuses in the field nearby. Something must have happened to him!"

Annette and her father looked at each other.

"The path from the forest leads through the crocus fields and I've seen no sign of him," said Father.

Annette slipped her hand into her father's.

"Perhaps he has wandered into the forest to look for you," she said reassuringly. "Let's go and look for him. Klaus will probably be about somewhere to show us which direction he's gone in. Klaus hates long walks."

Together they set out up the hill towards the forest. They went in silence, for Father was afraid to voice his thoughts. He knew that the spring brought certain dangers to mountains in Switzerland – swollen torrents and sudden falls of melting snow called avalanches. And Dani was such a tiny boy.

Grandmother, left alone, went indoors and prayed. As she prayed she saw a picture, for the less Grandmother saw with her outward eyes the more she saw with her mind. And this time there seemed to rise before her the picture of a dark forest, furrowed by deep rushing streams, its paths rough with boulders and blocked with avalanches. Along this path ran Dani with his hands full of crocuses. Beside him walked an angel with white wings. In the shadow of those wings there was shelter and warmth and safety.

"'I promise you that their angels are always with my Father in heaven'," whispered Grandmother. "That's what Jesus said, isn't it? Yes, Dani has one of God's angels looking after him." And she rose from her knees feeling quite peaceful.

There was still no sign of Dani or Klaus in the fields, nor at the edge of the pinewoods. Up and down they searched, calling Dani's name, but nothing answered except the echoes of their voices and the rushing of the torrent. Gradually the sun sank towards the peaks and the shadows grew longer on the fields.

"Papa," said Annette suddenly, "I wonder if he has gone down to Lucien's house. I have seen Lucien talking to him once or twice. I will run down to their chalet and ask."

Over the drifts and the grass she bounded and reached Madame Morel's chalet in less than five minutes. The back door stood open, and Annette put her head round.

"Madame!" she called. "Lucien! Are you there? Have you seen Dani?"

The house was silent and deserted, yet they could not have gone far for they had left the door wide open. Annette was about to run across to the barns when she caught sight of Madame Morel's stout figure toiling up the track that led to their own chalet. Annette ran to meet her.

"Madame," she cried, catching hold of her hand, "have you seen our little Dani? He has run away, and we have not seen him for two hours. Do you think he might be with Lucien? Where is Lucien?"

"He may well be," answered Madame Morel rather grimly. "I have just been down to your chalet to ask if you could give me any news of Lucien. The lazy boy should have been home long ago, and the cows are crying out to be milked. I shall have to do it myself, unless he has arrived while I was away. If so, he will have gone straight to the shed. Let us go across and see."

They went together over to the barn and opened the heavy wooden door. A red cow was stamping and twitching her tail, but there was no Lucien to be seen. Madame turned away with an exclamation of annoyance. She was just about to close the door, when Annette seized hold of her sleeve and held up her finger.

"Listen!" she whispered, "what's that noise up in the loft?"

They both stood listening intently for a moment. From the straw dump above came the unmistakable sound of a child's stifled sobs.

Annette was up the ladder in an instant like a little wild cat, and Madame Morel lumbered up behind her. Both knew that something was desperately wrong, but Annette thought only of Dani and Madame thought only of Lucien.

"Lucien," cried Madame, "my poor child, what is the matter? Are you hurt?"

Annette seized the boy by the arm and shook him. "Where's Dani? You know, don't you? What have you done with him? Give him back!"

Lucien cowered lower in the straw, and shook his head violently.

"I don't... know... where... he... is," he sobbed. "It wasn't my fault."

"What wasn't your fault?" Annette screamed, shaking him harder. "Where is he? You do know! You're telling lies! Madame, make him speak the truth!"

Madame dragged Annette out of the way and knelt down by Lucien. Her face was very white. By now she had guessed that some harm had come to Dani and that Lucien knew of it. She pulled his face up from the straw, and turned it towards her.

"Lucien," she commanded, trying to speak quietly, "speak at once. Where is Dani?"

Lucien stared at her wildly and saw that escape was impossible.

"He's dead," he said with a hiccup. He began to cry again with his head buried in the straw.

Annette had heard, but she did not move. Just for a few moments she had lost all power of movement. Her face was so ashen in the dim light that Madame thought she was going to faint, and tried to put her arms round her. But Annette sprang away. Then she spoke in a hoarse voice that did not sound like her own any longer.

"He must come and show us where," she said at last. "And at least my father can carry him home. And later," she added, slowly, "I will kill Lucien."

Madame took no notice of the last part of this speech, but the first suggestion sounded sensible. She took her boy by the arm, dragged him to his feet and almost carried him down the ladder.

"Come, Lucien," she urged at the bottom, "you must show us where Dani is, quickly. Otherwise Monsieur Burnier will be here with the police."

This threat frightened a little bit of sense and reason into Lucien. He set off up the hill as fast as he could go, sobbing all the time and crying that it was not his fault. Madame Morel and Annette followed. Madame Morel was sobbing as well, but Annette could not shed one tear. She felt as though all her tears were frozen up by rage and misery.

They reached the wall very quickly and Lucien pointed over into the darkening ravine. "He is over there, drowned in the torrent," he whispered, and then flung himself down and buried his face in the grass. At this moment, Monsieur Burnier appeared at the edge of the wood and hurried towards the little group.

He took no notice of Lucien. He took one look at his daughter and one look at the rocks, and in that quick glance he saw something that none of the others had noticed. He saw a shivering white kitten crouching on a ledge, right on the crest of the overhanging boulder. Once he had seen this, no more words were needed for the moment. He simply said, "I must fetch a rope," and ran down the mountain like a man being chased by wild animals.

Grandmother was at the door of the chalet, and she saw written in his face all that she needed to know at that moment. Without a word, she watched him pull down his climbing rope that hung on the wall and bound away into the shadows.

"In the ravine," he suddenly called back; and then he disappeared.

Grandmother, left alone, put on a kettle. She fetched old linen and filled a large stone hot-water bottle, so as to be ready for anything. Then she sat down and shut her eyes and folded her hands. Once again she saw a picture of Dani, caught by the dark waters of the ravine. But the white wings of the angel stemmed the current and Dani was caught up safely into his arms.

"'God will command his angels to protect you wherever you go'," whispered Grandmother. She climbed the stairs to turn down Dani's little bed and warm the blankets.

Dani's father was back with the rope in an amazingly short time, but to the watchers by the wall it seemed like hours. Nobody spoke as he secured it round a tree trunk and flung it over the boulder. Then, gripping it with his hands and knees, he slid down the slippery rocks and disappeared into the ravine. There, hanging in space, he dared to look down towards the rushing waters that must surely have carried away his child. And what he saw sent a great rush of hope into his heart, and a cry to his lips.

For Grandmother had seen right. The angels had taken care of Dani as he fell, and he had never reached the water at all. He had fallen onto a jutting-out boulder. There he lay, flat on his back, with his leg doubled up under him, waiting for someone to come and rescue him. He was crying because he could not move. The time had been long and Dani supposed he had been to sleep, for he could never remember much about those two hours afterwards. He really remembered only the moment when his father hovered over him like some big bird, and then knelt on the rock at his side.

"Papa," whispered Dani, a little faintly, "where's Klaus?"

"Just above you," replied his father. "We'll pick her up on the way back."

"Papa," went on Dani, "my leg hurts and I can't move. Will you carry me home?"

"Of course," replied his father. "That is what I've come for. I'll carry you home at once." And he took his little son in his arms.

"But Papa," went on the anxious, feeble voice, "can you carry us both, Klaus and me together? You won't leave Klaus, will you? Because it's time she had her milk and she'll be very thirsty."

"Klaus shall go in my pocket," promised his father, and he lifted the child very, very gently. Dani moaned, for his leg hurt dreadfully when moved. But he kept his eyes on his father's face and was really as brave as it is possible to be at 5 years old.

It was a long, slow journey back. Dani's father could not climb the rope with Dani in his arms. He had to scramble down to the edge of the torrent and pick his way along the side of it until they came to a part where the bank was less steep. Here, he was able to make his way up. Dani sank into a sort of deep sleep, and seemed to know nothing until his father laid him down on the grass beside Annette.

"Have you got Klaus in your pocket?" said Dani, opening his eyes suddenly.

"I'm fetching her now," replied his father. Holding on to the rope, he slid to the edge of the precipice again and picked up the white kitten. Dani held out his arms and Klaus nestled down against his heart, purring wildly. And Annette, for the first time in all that nightmare evening, burst into tears.

They laid him on a coat and Madame Morel and Monsieur Burnier carried him slowly home down the mountain, while Annette came behind carrying Klaus. They were a sad little procession, and yet their hearts were full of gratitude. Dani was alive, and had spoken. That for the moment was enough.

And no one, not even his mother, gave one thought to Lucien, who still lay under the wall, huddled down in the grass. When he lifted his head and found that he had been left alone with the night, he felt as though the whole world had cast him out and forgotten him. He got up, slunk home through the shadows and crept, shivering, to bed, as lonely and miserable a little boy as ever walked this earth.

7

Dani lay in his little bed between hot blankets. He was fully aware of the fact that he was a tremendously important person, and that anything he chose to ask for would be fetched immediately. He liked that feeling a lot.

Father stood at the end of the bed watching him and telling him all the funny stories he liked best. Annette sat on one side of him with a chocolate stick in her hand. Klaus was curled up on his chest purring. Grandmother sat the other side with a bowl of cherry jam, and every time he asked for it she gave him a spoonful! If his leg had not been aching so, Dani would have thought he was in heaven. But even though it hurt, Dani thought the cherry jam more than made up for the pain.

"Papa," said Dani, for about the tenth time, "are you quite, quite certain Klaus isn't hurt?"

"Quite certain," answered his father. "She drank a whole dish of milk, and ran upstairs with her tail up. Only healthy kittens would behave like that."

"Papa," went on Dani, opening his mouth like a baby bird for another mouthful of cherry jam, "it was Lucien who threw Klaus over the wall. Papa, it was very cruel of Lucien, wasn't it?"

"Very," replied his father, "and he shall certainly be punished." But Monsieur Burnier was too happy to have his son alive to think very much about Lucien. It was Annette, sitting quietly by, who thought most about Lucien.

I shall not be in a hurry, thought Annette to herself, but I shall never, never forgive him as long as I live. One day I shall do something terrible to him. I shall never forgive him, never.

"Nette," said Dani, "I want my chocolate stick, and then I want to go to sleep. And you must stay with me, Nette, because my leg hurts."

"Yes, Dani," answered Annette, handing him the chocolate stick. "I'll stay with you till you go to sleep."

Papa and Grandmother kissed him and left the room. Annette drew his head against her arm.

"Sing to me," commanded Dani. "Sing, '*Oh que Ta main paternelle, Me bénisse à mon coucher*'." It was Dani's little evening prayer that his grandmother had taught him. It was a prayer asking the Father in heaven to forgive all the wrong things done and said and thought during the day. The prayer also asked God to shelter little children under his wings for the night. Annette had often sung it before, but tonight she didn't want to. She could not really sing about forgiving wrongs when her heart was so full of hatred to Lucien that she could think of nothing but revenge.

"Not that one," said Annette. "I'll sing you another one about the bridge of Avignon. You say that other one to yourself, Dani."

Dani pouted. Tonight Annette ought to do whatever he wanted.

"I want '*Oh que Ta main paternelle*'," he said.

"Oh, all right," said Annette with a little sigh. "I'll sing it if you like." And she sang it rather sadly. The first verses go like this in French:

Oh! que Ta main paternelle
Me bénisse à mon coucher!
Et que ce soit sous ton aile
Que je dorme, ô mon Berger.

Veuille effacer par ta grâce
Les péchés que j'ai commis
Et que ton Esprit me fasse
Obéissant et soumis.

Oh, may the hand of my Father,
Bless me as I go to sleep,
And beneath your wings of shelter
May your little children keep.

Will you forgive by your grace, Lord,
All wrong things I've done today.
May your Holy Spirit make me
Kind and ready to obey.
(English translation)

The tune was slow and haunting. By the time Annette had finished, Dani was fast asleep, dribbling out his chocolate stick onto the pillow. She laid her hand down beside him. Once again she wept, for she was very tired and the relief had been so great.

She got up with a sigh and went downstairs. Her father was out with the cows, which had never been milked so late before in their lives. They were lowing and stamping with indignation. Grandmother was preparing something to eat, for neither she nor Monsieur Burnier had had a bite to eat since dinner. No one had had time to think of anything but Dani.

"He's asleep," said Annette. She sat down and stared listlessly into the stove.

"The doctor should be here soon," said Grandmother, "and then we shall have to wake him, poor little man. Never mind. Let him sleep while he can."

"Grandmother," said Annette, looking up suddenly after a little silence, "Lucien must be punished. What is to be done to him? I can think of nothing that would pay him back for doing such an evil thing."

The grandmother did not answer for a time. Then she replied, "Have you ever thought, Annette, that when we do wrong it often brings its own punishment without anyone else interfering?"

No, Annette had never thought about it at all.

"Think of Lucien's fright when he saw Dani fall," went on Grandmother. "Think of his misery and remorse tonight. Think of his shame and fear of others finding out what he did. And then think whether perhaps he has not been punished enough, and whether we should forgive him and help him to start again."

Annette did not take much notice of Grandmother's words, except for one sentence. "Think of his shame and fear of others finding out what he did." That was a great idea. She would see to it that they found out. Wherever she went she would tell everybody. She would tell it in the village and tell it at school, until everyone would hate him for what he'd done to Dani.

Her thoughts were interrupted by a hurried knock at the door and Lucien's big sister burst into the room. She worked in the town across the mountain and had arrived home just in time to meet the slow little procession coming down from the fields. She had sped down to the village post office to phone the doctor who lived five miles up the valley.

"Dr Pilliard can't come," she panted. "He has gone to another village to a sick woman and he won't be home till midnight and the last train's gone. They say you must take Dani in the cart to the hospital tomorrow morning and he will see him there."

"Thank you, Marie," said Grandmother. "It was good of you to go for us." She turned away. But Marie hesitated.

"Tell me, Annette," she said, lowering her voice, "how did the accident happen? Why was my mother so silent and troubled?"

"It happened up the mountain," replied Annette shortly. "Lucien threw Dani's kitten over the ravine, and Dani tried to rescue her. Lucien did not try to stop Dani at all. I shouldn't wonder if he pushed him. I think Dani has broken his leg. He lay on the rocks for hours and Lucien never told anybody."

Marie went pale with horror, for she had never been particularly fond of her young brother. If she had been, perhaps Lucien might have turned out a better, kinder boy. Children who are not loved are seldom loving.

"He'll be severely punished," she said angrily; "I will see to it myself." Then she flounced out of the house. Annette smiled. To turn his own family against Lucien was just what Annette wanted. She felt her revenge had begun.

There was nothing more to wait for now. So, after a rather silent meal, Annette dragged her way up to bed, tired and heavy-hearted. She lit a candle and stood looking at Dani through eyes that were misty with tears. He lay with his damp hair pushed back from his forehead and his arms flung out. His usual peaceful look had gone. He was frowning even in his sleep, and now and then he moved his head restlessly and muttered troubled words.

Annette got into her bed by the window, but tired as she was, she could not sleep. She felt strangely alone. Then, to her joy, she heard slow, painful steps climbing the stairs and Grandmother came into the room – Grandmother who hardly ever came upstairs because it hurt her rheumaticky leg so badly.

"Grandma!" cried Annette. She held out her arms.

Grandmother said nothing for a time. She sat down on the bed and stroked Annette's head until the girl stopped crying.

"Listen, my child," said Grandmother at last, "when Dani was a baby we took him to the church and by faith we laid him in the arms of the Saviour. Every day in prayer we have asked the Saviour to hold him safe in his arms. And even when Dani fell, the Saviour did not let go of him. His arms were underneath him all the time. Even if he had been killed he would have been carried straight home to heaven. So let us dry our tears and go on trusting the Saviour to hold Dani, and do the very best for him."

"But why did God let Lucien hurt him so?" asked Annette. "Grandma, I hate Lucien so much I want to kill him."

"Then you cannot pray for Dani," replied Grandmother simply. "God is love, and when we pray we are drawing near to love. So all our hatred must melt away, like the snow melts when the sun shines on it in spring. Leave Lucien to God, Annette. He rewards both good and evil. But remember, he loves Lucien just the same as he loves Dani."

Grandmother kissed her and went away, and Annette lay thinking over Grandmother's words. The last remark she did not believe. It seemed impossible that even God should love cruel, stupid Lucien as much as good, sunny little Dani. But the first part she knew to be true, and it troubled her. She could not really pray for Dani and go on planning how to hurt Lucien. The two just did not go together. She wanted to pray for Dani, but if she did, her hatred might disappear and she did not want that to happen at all. Anyhow, not before she had really had her revenge.

Well, in the meantime she would let Grandmother do the praying and she would go on planning her revenge. And, just as she decided this, Dani sat up in bed and started crying in a frightened half asleep sort of way.

"Klaus!" cried Dani. "Where's Klaus? She's fallen into the river."

Annette went over to him. "No, no," she murmured, "she's here!" She picked up the white purring ball of fur, and put it in Dani's arms. He fell asleep again, with his kitten sprawling across his chest.

Annette waited beside him for a few minutes until his breathing grew quiet and peaceful. Then she climbed into bed and fell asleep too.

8

Lucien also lay in bed in the dark, with a hot throbbing head and eyes that could not shut. Each time he closed them, he saw Dani disappearing over the edge of the ravine. And it wasn't the ordinary ravine, it was a dark, sheer cliff that had no bottom. Lucien knew if you fell, you just went on falling for ever and ever.

Now and again he half fell asleep. But each time he awoke with a little cry of fear and his heart beating wildly, for his dreams were even worse than his thoughts. If only someone would come! It was so dreadful being alone. He wanted his mother. He could hear her moving about in the kitchen below. But he dared not call to her, for he thought she must be so angry. Perhaps that was why she was staying away from him. Besides, his sister might answer his call, and Lucien did not in the least want to see his sister. What she would say to him he dared not even imagine.

He began to think about tomorrow. He supposed he would have to go to school and Annette would have told everyone. Nobody liked him much in any case. They said he was bad-tempered and stupid, but at least they let him play with them. Now they would all hate him. No one would be friends, or want to sit next to him in class.

He heard steps on the stair, and his mother came into the room. He sat up, crying, and held out his arms to her. But she did not come to him. Instead, she sat down on the bed and watched him with a worried frown.

All her heart went out to him in pity, and she longed to comfort him, but she was dreadfully frightened. She was afraid of what the Burniers would do if Dani were badly injured. She was afraid of the law, afraid of doctors' bills that she could not pay. Besides, she felt it her duty to punish her son somehow.

If she had been an understanding woman she would have seen that no punishment of hers was needed. She would have seen the long weeks of fear and loneliness and remorse that lay ahead of Lucien, and she would have known that her part was to comfort him and help him through them as best she might. But she was not very understanding.

"You are a naughty boy, Lucien," she said heavily, "and I do not know what is going to happen. If that Burnier child is badly injured we shall be ruined. We shall have to pay all the bills, and we cannot possibly afford it. I shouldn't wonder if we get the police after us. It's a terrible thing to have done, and I hope you are heartily ashamed of yourself."

Lucien was so very ashamed of himself that he didn't answer at all. This puzzled his mother very much, for Lucien was usually so quick to answer back and to stick up for himself. A silent Lucien was indeed a new thing.

"Well," she said at last in a gentler voice, "we must hope for the best! Tomorrow you could go and tell the Burniers how sorry you are, and perhaps they will forgive you."

She waited for his reply, but none came, so she said no more and left the room very troubled. She returned presently with a bowl of hot soup. She thought she should punish her son but she just couldn't see him go hungry.

Lucien took the bowl and tried to eat, but at the third mouthful he choked and handed it back to his mother. Then, flinging himself down with his face buried in the pillows, he cried again as though his heart would break. His mother said nothing, for she did not know what to say. She stroked the back of his head gently, and then as his sobs grew quieter she crept away and left him to the night.

When he awoke next morning he could not remember what had happened, nor why his head ached and his eyes felt hot and heavy. Then it all came rushing back like a blow, and he remembered something else too. Today he had got to go to school and face the other children.

Dani might have died in the night and they would all know it was his fault.

Lucien decided he would not go, he would hide all day. It would not be very difficult. He would run up to the pinewoods and come back late in the afternoon, and no one would ever know. His mother would think he had been at school and no one from school would ask questions. He lived too far up the valley, and, besides, who cared? Of course, someone would find out in the end, but today was all that mattered at the moment. He might feel different tomorrow, or Dani might be better. Anything might happen later on, but today he would run away and hide.

He got up and went downstairs. Marie was in the kitchen. She had already eaten her bread and drunk her coffee and was getting ready to set out for the station. She tossed her head and turned away when Lucien came in, but Lucien took no notice. He passed through the kitchen in silence, and went across to the stable to help his mother with the early milking.

His mother watched him with a troubled expression when he came in, but he said nothing. And later, sitting on his stool by the stove, eating his breakfast, he was still silent. At last he got up, buttoned on his coat, kissed his mother goodbye without a word and went off.

She stood watching him as far as the bend and then waved to him. He waved back and waited round the corner until he was sure she had gone. Then he scudded up the hill as fast as his legs would carry him.

He ran very fast, and arrived breathless into the quiet coolness of the great pinewood that skirted the mountain. Here he was safe, for it was still early morning (school began at 7.30am), so he sat down and began to think.

It was a beautiful pinewood and the trees, wakening at the call of spring, were surging with sap and scent. The sap burst from them and streamed down their grey trunks. A sweet hot smell rose from the ground where the sun, filtering through the boughs, shone in patches on the pine needles. The forest seemed full of peace and cool light. Lucien suddenly felt a tiny bit hopeful, as though one of the stray sunbeams had lost its way among the boughs and had pierced the misery in his heart.

He had no idea what he was going to do all day. He had no food, as dinner was always provided for him in the school dining room. But this strange feeling of hope made him feel sleepy. Because he had spent a broken, troubled night, he stretched himself on the needles, well hidden by some wild raspberry bushes, and fell into a deep sleep.

The warm spring winds ruffled his hair and the stray sunbeams kissed him from time to time. Busy little grey squirrels chattered in the treetops and pelted cones at each other, and the stream in the hollow laughed its way over the stones. But Lucien slept on until the sun was high overhead and the children down in the school were coming out to eat their dinners. Then he woke up and wanted his dinner, too.

But there was none to be had here in the forest. He got up and wandered on up the hill, wondering whether some kindly farmer in one of the higher chalets might give him a drink of milk. And as he wandered he stuck his hands in his pockets and found his knife.

He had come to the edge of that part of the forest now. Beeches grew among the pines, and steep grass slopes rose in front of him. The beech buds were fat and ready to burst, and here and there a feathery leaf had pushed through. Soon they would all burst into life and the forest would look like a cathedral, with tender green tracery against a blue sky.

Lucien sat down again on a log and picked up a piece of wood. He began whittling at it with his knife. He had often whittled at bits of wood, but he hadn't really made anything. But now, with nothing to do, he decided to try to carve out the shape of a chamois, one of the wild mountain goats that live on the high precipices. He started off idly, chipping away at the wood.

Very gradually it began to take shape under his fingers, and a strange excitement took hold of him. For the first time he forgot his misery and began to get really interested in what he was doing. He could see the creature in his mind's eye, and his fingers followed his thoughts. A head with beautiful curved horns and an eager tilted nose was beginning to appear. Then four slender hooves, and a body poised for flight.

Lucien held it out at arm's length to inspect it. It was not perfect, though it was an unmistakable likeness. Lucien himself had no idea how good it was. But for the first time since the accident he felt almost happy. He had found something he could do. Stupid as he was, he could carve, and now he would not mind being alone again. When the other children didn't want him, he would come out to a quiet corner of the woods and see beautiful things and carve them. While he carved he could forget, and that was what he wanted more than anything. Whatever happened, he could come away by himself and forget.

He climbed up the slope and looked down over the forest to the valley below. The sun was moving towards the western mountains, and far beneath he could see little dark specks running in all directions. The children were coming out of school. In another quarter of an hour or so it would be safe to go home.

He sauntered slowly back through the pinewood, for he must not get back too soon. The sun was shining on the other side of the valley now, and the pinewood was cool and dark and filled with little wakeful murmurs. Lucien kept his hand in his pocket with his fingers closed tightly over the rounded body of his chamois. It was a satisfying feeling.

He wondered rather dully what he would hear when he got home. Dani might have died. Lucien pushed that thought away from him, for he dared not face it. He was probably just badly hurt. Into Lucien's mind there came a picture of Dani's white, scared little face looking up from the grass.

If only he could do something to make up for what had happened. But he could think of nothing.

He walked into the chalet a little sheepishly, and his mother, at the sink, eyed him anxiously. She waited a little while for him to speak. But at last, unable to contain her curiosity any longer, she began to question him.

"Well," she began, "how did you get on at school today?"

"All right, thank you," answered Lucien.

"I've been down to the Burniers'," went on his mother, "and Annette and Monsieur have taken Dani to the doctor in the cart. They will not be back till late. The grandmother spoke very kindly, Lucien. They are good people and I think they will forgive you and not make the trouble you deserve."

Lucien didn't reply. The grandmother might forgive him, but he knew quite well that Annette never would.

"Did the schoolmaster know of what had happened?" asked his mother after a pause.

"Yes," replied Lucien.

"Did he say anything about it?"

"No."

His mother was puzzled. She had had a miserable day thinking of what her son might be suffering at school, but nothing seemed to have happened. He even looked slightly more cheerful than he had looked in the morning.

"I am going over to milk, Mother," said Lucien. And he crossed to the stable with a sigh of relief. The stable was a refuge where he could get away from his mother's questions, and where the cows thought none the worse of him. He started quickly. Then, tilting the bucket, he drank about a pint of warm frothing milk straight off and felt better.

Tonight he would save some of his supper, and tomorrow he would go back to the woods again and spend another quiet, hidden day. He would do it every day till he was found out. That might not be for a long time.

He took as long as he could over the milking and then sauntered back to the house carrying the pails. He reached the door at the same time as his sister, who had hurried up the hill and was flushed and breathless.

"You little coward, Lucien!" she exclaimed, by way of greeting. "Fancy missing school like that! What has he been doing all day, Mother? You should have made him go!"

Her mother turned round indignantly. "What are you talking about, Marie?" she asked sharply. "Of course he's been to school. He's only just come in. Leave the poor child alone and get on with your work."

"Indeed!" exclaimed Marie. "Well, if he's only just come in, I should like to know where he's come from. I met the schoolmaster on my way up from the station. He called out to me. 'Where's Lucien?' he said. 'And why has he not come to school? Is he not well?' And I answered, 'He's well enough, and he shall come tomorrow, if I have to drag him!' So now you know, Lucien! Goodness knows where you've been today, but tomorrow I shall take you to school myself."

"How could you lie to me like that, Lucien?" cried his mother angrily. "You are a terrible boy. I don't know what to do with you. The master must deal with you." And because she was so worried, and because her boy had deceived her, she threw her apron over her face and began to cry.

Lucien sat down by the stove in bitter, sullen silence. Everything and everyone seemed against him. His only hope of escape had been taken from him. Tomorrow he would have to go to school and Annette would be there. If he had gone today she would not have been there.

He picked up a large chip and began whittling away with his knife. And once more his fingers felt for the wooden chamois in his pocket.

9

Dani lay in the cart on a sack stretched across a soft mattress of hay and gazed up at the sky, where tiny white woolly clouds floated like sleepy lambs in a blue meadow. He would have liked to look over the sides of the cart, but this was impossible, for he could not sit up. So he looked at the sky instead, and Annette described the scenery and events of their journey. Dani's leg ached badly, and when the cart jolted he squealed. But Annette soothed him with her talk.

"We're at the top of the village now, Dani," said Annette, "just passing the church, and there is Emil the dustman's son driving the cows out of the churchyard. Some silly person must have left the gate open."

"Are the cows trying to go into church?" Dani said with interest.

"No," replied Annette. "They were trying to jump over the wall, but it was too high. They were jumping over the gravestones instead. Here we are at the infant school, Dani, and there is the mistress scrubbing her step. I suppose it is her cleaning day and she has given all the infants a holiday. I wish the master had cleaning days. Oh! The mistress is coming towards the cart. She has seen us, and I expect she wants to know how you are! And here come Madame Pilet and Madame Lenoir. They have seen us, too. They were washing their clothes in the fountain."

Annette was right. They certainly wanted to know how Dani was. For in their tiny village news travelled fast and was much talked of and long remembered because there was so little of it. The postman's wife had heard some of the story from Lucien's sister when she phoned for the doctor. The stationmaster's wife had heard the rest from

Marie while she waited for the early train. By now everyone knew about what had happened to Dani. Everyone was talking about it and everyone wanted to find out more.

So Madame Pilet and Madame Lenoir left their husbands' shirts bubbling like white balloons in the fountain. And Madame Duruz who kept the village shop left her counter and came running out with her two customers behind her. The schoolmistress left her scrubbing bucket to get cold. And they all crowded round the cart and stood on tiptoe to stare at Dani, lying flat on his back on his hay mattress. He was a little paler than usual, but otherwise, they agreed, he seemed quite happy and pleased to see them.

"Ah, the poor little thing!" cried the mistress, and threw up her hands. "You must tell us about it, Annette." And although they had all heard the story once and had all repeated it to somebody else, they were all ready to listen again. So Annette told them about it, and they shook their heads a great deal, and clicked their tongues. They were loud in their indignation against poor Lucien.

"He is a horrible boy," said the schoolmistress, "I shall warn the little children not to have anything to do with him!"

"I shall not allow Pierre to play with him," said the postman's wife. "He has a cruel heart. You can see it in his face. I am sorry for his mother." She spoke in a superior way, and thought proudly of her own merry-faced, freckled Pierre, who was one of the best-loved boys in the village.

Dani's father flicked his whip a little impatiently, and said that they must not keep the doctor waiting. So the women stood back and the cart lumbered on slowly over the cobbles. Then they all drew together again and started talking in the middle of the road with their heads very close together.

The cart jolted on and the sun rose higher. The horse did not mind in the least about keeping the doctor waiting. So Annette had plenty of time to describe the scenery to Dani as they made their way, slowly, to town. On their left, the mountains rose steeply upward. On their right, there was a low stone wall. Behind it, the mountain sloped steeply downwards and plunged straight into the river.

"The river is almost in flood, Dani," remarked Annette. "It is because the fine weather has melted the snows so fast. The water is right over the pine roots, and here a tree has fallen right across like a bridge – and oh, Dani! There is a little grey squirrel wondering whether to run along it or not."

"Where?" cried Dani. He forgot about his leg and tried to rise, but fell back with a squeal of pain.

"You can't see," Annette warned him. "And anyhow the squirrel has run back into the wood. We are getting near the station now, Dani. There are three cows on the platform waiting to be put on the train."

The journey passed pleasantly. They left the great roaring waterfall behind on their right hand, and went on up a broad road, with young mountain ash trees on either side. They passed by the sawmills with machines smelling of sawdust, and then on between fields of young crocuses, until houses began to appear. Annette told Dani that they were coming to the town.

"Tell me about the shops!" said Dani eagerly.

He had been to the town only three times in his short life, and thought it the most wonderful place in the world.

It wasn't much of a town, with only one narrow street of shops. But they were very nice shops. There was the cake shop with its windows packed with flat fruit tarts and piles of gingerbread cut into every imaginable shape. And there was the clothes shop with its display of flounced embroidered national costumes. Best of all was the woodcarvers' shop with its rows of carved cuckoo clocks, and wooden men who opened their mouths wide and cracked nuts in their teeth. Annette was quite breathless with describing the beauties of this shop, when at last they drove up in front of the hospital.

It was only a little hospital really, but to Annette and Dani, it seemed enormous. The patients all lay out on sunny balconies, and the door was wide open. Father jumped down from the driver's seat, tied the reins to the fence and went in. A few minutes later he returned with two men and a stretcher.

Dani was laid on the stretcher. Then he was taken to a wooden bench in the outpatients' hall, and lay there quite still, with Father sitting at his head and Annette at his feet. The quiet strangeness of the place and the odd, clean smell awed them all into silence. So Dani watched the nurses instead. They wore long white aprons and lace caps. Dani thought they were exactly like the angels in Grandmother's big picture Bible.

They waited for a very long time. Father and Annette nodded and dozed. Dani flung his arms above his head and fell into a deep sleep.

He was woken by the doctor who bore down on them very suddenly and seemed in a great hurry. He was an elderly man with a large black beard and a gruff voice.

Everything seemed to happen very quickly after that. Dani was hustled off on a trolley to have the bones of his leg photographed. This was interesting, and he wanted to know whether he would be allowed to keep the photograph to hang up in the living room. Then he was trundled back, and the doctor pulled the bad leg till Dani screamed with pain. At this point, the photographs were brought along, not looking in the least like Dani's legs. But the doctor seemed pleased with them. He studied them deeply and nodded his head wisely. Then he turned to Father and remarked, "This child should stay in hospital. He has broken his leg very badly."

But Annette's father refused. He was not going to leave his little son to this man with his black beard and his hands that were none too gentle. "We will look after Dani at home," he said firmly. "Surely that is possible?"

The doctor shrugged his shoulders. "It is possible," he replied, "but I think he would be better here. I cannot come so far. You would have to keep bringing him in."

"I do not mind bringing him in," said Father obstinately. Annette stole her little hand into his big one and gave it an approving squeeze. She, too, wanted Dani at home.

The doctor shrugged his shoulders again and spread out his hands. Dani was once more trundled off by a nurse in a great hurry, and this time he did not come back for more than half an hour.

When at last he was returned to them, he looked sleepy and strange and could remember absolutely nothing but an odd smell. He did not realise at first that he was encased from his waist to his knee in a fine white plaster. But Annette soon pointed this out to him and Dani stared down at himself in astonishment.

"Why have I got to wear these hard white trousers?" he asked at last. "And why have these trousers only got one leg?" Then, without waiting for a reply, he announced that he did not like the doctor's big black beard and he wanted to go home.

Annette did not like it either, and was a little afraid of the doctor. They all wanted to go home – Annette because she was hungry, Dani because he was tired, and Father because he was thinking about his cows. When the doctor came back to take a second photograph, Dani and his family were nowhere to be seen. In the far distance, a sprightly horse was making his way towards home as fast as possible, trundling a hay cart and three passengers behind him.

"Stupid creatures," muttered the doctor. "I suppose they thought I was never coming back. Now I shall have to trudge up some out-of-the-way mountain for the best part of a day and visit the child. They did not even wait to hear when they were to come again."

Actually, they had quite forgotten to ask. But then, Father remembered.

"Annette," he called to his daughter, "we never asked how long Dani had to wear his plaster."

"Never mind," Annette answered. "You will be passing again with the cheeses in a week's time and you can call in and ask them. You may be sure it will have to stay on as long as that. Leon at school had one on his arm and he wore it six weeks."

"So he did!" replied Father, reassured. "Then I won't turn back now, for it is getting late. Anyway, that doctor was nowhere in sight." And the horse began to trot even faster, as keen to get home as his passengers were.

They reached home at five o'clock and Dani was put to bed on the sofa so that he might not feel lonely. Annette slept on a mattress beside him in case he should wake in the night and want her. Here Dani stayed for weeks, with his leg on a pillow, and the whole household moved round him.

Annette stopped going to school altogether for the time being, and gave herself up to being Dani's servant. She told him all her stories over and over again and played games with him all day long. Grandmother cooked wonderful little meals to tempt the appetite of the "poor little sick boy". Dani's appetite didn't need tempting in the least, for he was almost as cheery and hungry on his couch as he was off it. Sometimes they moved the sofa out onto the veranda, so he could at least get some fresh air. So when Annette was busy he would lie flat on his back on the veranda bed and sing like a happy lark.

He certainly had everything to make him happy; the village saw to that. They had loved his pretty, delicate mother who had grown up amongst them. When she died they were all prepared to love her children. They especially loved Dani, with his twinkling eyes like forget-me-nots and his happy nature.

Dani was so very pleased and excited by the many wonderful presents and visits, he scarcely missed his freedom at first.

There were the children, for instance, who wandered up the mountains in search of the first alpine flowers for him. Eventually, the table by his bed looked like an alpine garden. And because Dani loved to see them, Grandmother put up with the noise and the muddy boots. She tried to remain cheerful even though the veranda, out of school hours, became a sort of public playground... and a very noisy one too.

Then there was the schoolmaster who sent fascinating picture books, and the innkeeper who sent brown speckled eggs. And there was the baker who made golden doughboys with currant eyes and candied-peel buttons. He used to slip them in Annette's breadbasket with a wink, and that was why Dani always insisted on unpacking the shopping basket himself. He never knew what he might find. Whatever it was, he was quite certain it was for him.

But the postman was best of all. The Burnier family very seldom received a letter, and the arrival of the postman was always a great event. So he decided to write Dani a weekly picture postcard. He would toil up the hill to deliver it himself. As he chose a different day of the week every time, Dani looked forward to each morning, for he never knew when the postman would come.

The postman was never in a hurry, and always saw to it that the postcard was at the very bottom of the sack. He enjoyed Dani's squeals of excitement as the boy burrowed among the letters. Dani could read his own name, and carefully examined the names on all the cards in search of his own. And if the post that day was a little thumbed and crumpled no one minded or asked questions.

10

Just as the village rallied round Dani and did all they could to comfort him, so they shunned Lucien. They did all they could to show their contempt.

For the first few days he was really tormented. The master made a speech about him in school and held him up as a public example of a bully and a coward. The children chased him out of the playground and threw mud at him. But they soon gave that up and just ignored him.

Lucien had never been greatly liked, for he was bad-tempered and clumsy. But he had gone about with the crowd, and joined in with their games. Now he had to settle down to a terrible, dull, lasting loneliness. Nobody wanted to play with him. When teams were picked he was always left till last. There was one extra single desk in the classroom. Lucien sat there by himself. All the others sat in couples.

Even the tiny children got out of his way, for their mothers had warned them to have nothing to do with him. "He is a cruel bully and may harm you as he harmed little Daniel Burnier," said the mothers. So the little ones looked on him as a sort of ogre, and ran away as he approached.

Down at the village shops they handed him his goods across the counter silently. The milkman never chatted and joked with him as he used to do. The grocer's wife never slipped trimmings of gingerbread into his hand as she did to other children. The people never spoke unkindly to him. They just took no notice of him.

And Lucien, too shy to make any attempt to overcome their dislike, drifted into a lonely little world of his own.

He walked to and from school alone, he shopped alone, and in the playground he usually played alone. The children might have forgiven him more easily if he had been friendlier to them. But his shame kept him away from even trying. Always he saw hostility and dislike in their faces, and imagined they were thinking of poor Dani. Gradually he grew to be afraid of them. He became afraid of everyone, from the old milkman right down to the youngest child in the school. He was afraid of their scorn and dislike.

For Lucien himself was always thinking of Dani. The thought of what he had done haunted him, and he yearned to ask Annette what the doctor had said. But Annette had neither looked at him nor spoken to him since the day of the accident, and he dared not speak to her.

At home his mother found him more silent but more hard-working, for he had suddenly discovered that only by hard work could he forget his loneliness. So instead of indulging in his old lazy habits he threw himself into the work of the farm with an almost desperate energy. His mother praised him loudly, and his sister became kinder. Marie was a hard-working girl and Lucien's laziness had always annoyed her, but even she could see that now he was making an effort.

There was only one place, though, where Lucien was completely happy, and that was in the forest. Here the kindly trees shut him in, and the world that disliked him was shut out. Here Lucien fled whenever he had any spare time and, squatting against a tree trunk or boulder, he would carve away at his little figures and forget everything else.

The peace and beauty of the forest in early summer soothed and comforted him. The boulders were like moss gardens planted with cushions of starry saxifrage. The new baby cones on the pines were burnished and the beech leaves were at the tender, transparent stage when they seemed to sift rather than hide the light. Lucien, sitting beneath them, would feel the sun on his hair and hands as he worked.

High up on the borders of the forest there stood a small chalet where a very old man lived. He had retired there long ago and he lived alone with his goat, his hens, and his cat. He was a strange old man. Everyone in the village was afraid of him, and when he came down on rare occasions to shop, the children ran indoors. They called him the old man of the mountain. Some said he was a miser. Some said he was hiding from the police. Others said he was crazy. But these things were gossip and guesswork for no one had ever been inside his home… and no one ever passed that way after dark.

Lucien had wandered further than usual one half holiday and sat as usual intent on his work. He was carving a squirrel holding a nut between its paws when he suddenly became aware of someone behind him. He turned quickly to see the old man of the mountain looking over his shoulder.

He was certainly a terrifying sight. His huge matted grey beard covered his chest, and his hooked nose gave him the look of some fierce old bird of prey. But as Lucien gazed up, startled, he saw that the old man's eyes were bright and kindly and full of interest. Lucien decided not to run away. Besides, his great loneliness made him less afraid than he would have been otherwise. This old man might be very strange indeed, but at least he knew nothing about Lucien's past.

So Lucien said, "*Bonjour*, Monsieur," as boldly as he could, and waited to see what would happen next.

The old man put out a claw-like hand and picked up the little carved squirrel. He examined it and turned it over several times. Then he remarked, gruffly, "You carve well for a child. Who is your master?"

"Monsieur, I have no master. I taught myself."

"Then you yourself are a good master, and you deserve proper tools. With a little training you might start to earn your living. There is life in this squirrel."

"Monsieur, I have no tools, nor have I the money to buy them."

In reply the old man beckoned with his claw. Lucien, feeling like someone in a dream, rose and followed him through the dim wood. They climbed some way in silence until they came to the borders. Here stood the tiny chalet where the old man lived.

There was no outhouse except for a wood barn where the hens roosted. The goat shared the kitchen with the old man. So did the marmalade cat, who sat washing herself in the sunshine. The bedroom was also the hay loft, and the old man slept on sacks laid across the goat's winter fodder.

The kitchen and living room was poorly but strangely furnished. There was the stove, the milking bucket and stool, the manger, the table, one chair and a cheese press. But all round the walls, out of reach of the goat, were shelves covered with carved wooden figures. Some were beautiful, some were grotesque, but all were the work of a real artist.

There were bears and cows and chamois and goats and St Bernard dogs and squirrels. There were little men and women, gnomes and dwarfs, and dancing children. There were boxes with alpine flowers carved on their lids, and dishes with wreaths carved round the rim. And best of all there was a Noah's ark with a stream of tiny animals prancing in. Lucien could not take his eyes off this. He stared and stared and stared.

"Just a hobby of mine," said the old man. "They keep me company on winter evenings. Now, boy, if you will come and visit me from time to time, I will teach you the use of the tools."

Lucien looked up eagerly. His whole face was alive.

"Did you say, Monsieur," he asked hesitatingly, "that perhaps I might soon earn my living?"

"In time," said the old man, "yes. I have a friend who sells woodcraft at a good price. He sells many of my little figures. But some I get fond of and prefer to keep. In a short time he would start selling your best work for you. You will soon do much better with my tools than with your knife."

Still Lucien gazed up at him. His heart was singing with gratitude because this old man seemed to have taken an interest in him. Here at last was somebody of whom he need not be afraid, and who thought well of him.

"Oh, thank you, Monsieur," he cried. "How very good you are to me!"

"*Zut!*" said the old man. "I am lonely, and I have no friends. We can carve together."

"And I, too," replied Lucien simply, "am lonely, and have no friends."

As Lucien walked home through the forest his brain was seething with ideas. But there was one big idea more important than all the others. He would make a Noah's ark for Dani like the old man had done, with dozens of tiny figures – lions, rabbits, elephants, camels and cows, and Mr and Mrs Noah. When it was quite perfect, he would walk round to the Burniers' chalet and give it to Dani as a peace offering. Surely no one could give Dani a better present than that! And after that, perhaps – *perhaps* – they might even allow him to be friends with Dani.

His heart beat fast at the mere thought. For two whole hours he had been completely happy. His happiness lasted all the way through the forest until the trees parted and he saw the village spread out at his feet. Tomorrow he would have to go back to school. Tomorrow he would feel lonely and frightened again. But today he had kept company with a friend.

So three times a week after school Lucien bounded through the still pine forest. He sat on the step of the old man's chalet and worked at his Noah's ark. It was a wonderful thing to use those tools with their sharp blades and easy curves – very different from his old clasp knife.

The old man marvelled at the boy's skill. The Noah's ark family grew and multiplied. Every visit, Lucien thought of some new animal to carve, and the procession grew longer and longer.

Then, there was another excitement for Lucien. An inspector came to the school and set a handcraft competition for the children. The girls were to see who could enter the best specimen of knitting or needlework or lacemaking, and the boys the best specimen of woodcarving. Many of them whittled away at wood in their spare time, and some were well on the way to becoming skilful.

"But no one is as skilful as me," whispered Lucien to himself, as he plodded home alone. "I shall win the prize. And they will know that I can do something well, even if I am stupid at lessons, and even if no one will play with me."

Lucien sang on his way home that day. He saw himself walking up for his prize in front of the amazed school. Perhaps they would like him better after that.

He would carve a horse with a flowing mane, in full gallop, with tail outstretched and nostrils dilated. Lucien loved horses. The old man had carved one like that and Lucien had admired it tremendously. The Noah's ark would be finished very soon and then he could start on his little horse.

As soon as he could, he ran to the old man's house to share the news. The old man was pleased, and as sure of Lucien's success as Lucien was himself.

"But why try a horse?" he asked. "You could submit your Noah's ark. It is very well done for a boy of your age."

Lucien shook his head. "That is a present," he said firmly.

"A present? Who for? A little brother?"

"For a little child who has hurt himself and cannot walk."

"Indeed? How did he do that?"

"He fell over the ravine."

"Poor little fellow! How did that happen?"

Lucien did not answer for a moment. But the fact that this old man had befriended him and been nice to him made him want to speak the truth. He looked up at last and said, "It was my fault that he fell. I dropped his kitten over and he tried to get it."

He could have bitten his tongue out when he had said it. Now the old man would hate him and drive him away like everybody else.

But he didn't. Instead the old man said very gently, "So that is why you said you had no friends?"

"Yes."

"And you are trying to make amends to the child with this toy?"

"Yes."

"You are doing a good thing! It is hard work to win back love. But do not be discouraged. Those who persevere find more happiness in earning love than they do in gaining it."

"I don't quite understand you," said Lucien.

"I mean that if you spend your time putting the love of your heart into your deeds for those who are not your friends, you may often be disappointed and discouraged. But if you keep on you will find your happiness in loving, whether you are loved back or not. You may think it strange that I who live alone and love no one should say this. But I believe it all the same."

That evening the Noah's ark was finished and Lucien, with a flushed face and a hammering heart, set off for the Burniers' chalet to leave it on his way home.

When he came within sight of the chalet, he hid behind a tree in a panic. What would he say? How would he break the silence? If he could see Dani alone it would be easier, but Annette was always with him out of school hours.

Surely they would forgive him when they saw the Noah's ark! If only they would forgive him and give him a chance he would gladly spend the rest of his life trying to make up. And torn between hope and fear Lucien came out from behind the tree and walked towards the chalet.

Dani's bed had been carried in from where it had been set on the veranda. So Annette sat there alone, patching her father's jacket elbows. Lucien swallowed hard, walked up the steps and held out the Noah's ark.

"It's for Dani," he whispered hoarsely. Then his words stuck in his throat and he stood waiting with his eyes fixed on the ground.

Annette took the Noah's ark from him, her face white with fury.

"You dare come here!" she burst out at last. "You dare offer presents to Dani! Go away and don't you ever come here again!"

And as she said it she flung the Noah's ark with all her strength into the woodpile below. All the little animals lay scattered on the logs.

Lucien stared at her for a moment, then he turned and stumbled down the steps again. His efforts had been all for nothing. He would never be forgiven. It had all been one long waste of time.

And then the words of the old man came into Lucien's mind like a tiny ray of light in his angry, bitter heart.

"Those who persevere find more happiness in earning love than they do in gaining it."

Well, perhaps it was true. He had certainly not gained anything, but at least he had been happy making the Noah's ark, and thinking of Dani's pleasure. Perhaps, if he persevered and went on putting his love into his work, some day someone would accept it and love him for it.

He did not know… but he would not despair just yet.

11

Dani's leg was very slow in healing. On several occasions the doctor climbed the mountainside to visit him, but he seemed grave and puzzled. Then, when the narcissi were beginning to sprout in the fields, and the farmers were talking about taking the cows up the mountain, Dani went back to hospital and they took the plaster off. Then the doctor broke the bad news to Dani's father. As the doctor had feared all along, Dani would not be able to walk straight. The bad leg was shorter than the good one.

So, in very low spirits, Monsieur Burnier went to the carpenter and asked him to make a tiny pair of crutches. Then he visited the cobbler with a pair of Dani's boots and asked him to make one sole thicker than the other.

The carpenter and the shoemaker were dreadfully upset. The carpenter carved little bears' heads on the handle of the crutches in order to bring a smile to Dani's face. The cobbler returned the boots stuffed with chocolate sticks. And, in both cases, their efforts were a great success. Dani looked upon his crutches as a new toy, and was impatient to try them out.

For a day or two he hopped about like an excited grasshopper in front of the house. Then he heard his father say that he was going to take his cows up the mountain to feed in the high pastures. Then Dani sat down and bellowed, because he suddenly realised that even with his bear crutches and his chocolate boots he could no longer follow the cows up the mountain.

Dani did not often bellow, but when he did, he did it in real earnest. Annette, Monsieur Burnier, and Grandmother all rushed for the woodpile where Dani was crying. They all started shaking him and kissing him at once. Klaus, who hated a fuss, arched her back and hissed.

When at last they understood the cause of Dani's grief they were all full of comforting plans. In the end it was decided that Dani should go down to the marketplace in a little wood cart to watch the cows assemble. Afterwards, he could drive up behind the *troupeaux* in the horse cart, sleep the night in the hay, and come down next day. Annette would go with him, while Grandmother and Klaus stayed home.

The great day dawned clear and blue, and Dani woke early with a feeling that something wonderful was going to happen. When he remembered what it was he tried to yodel, which he couldn't do at all. Then he dragged Klaus into bed with him and began to tell her all about it. But Klaus wasn't interested and struggled out again and went with her tail in the air to catch mice on the woodpile.

An hour later, Dani was curled up in the wood cart and Annette was pulling him down to the village. Or rather, she was holding him back with all her might, for the path was steep and the cart really needed no pulling at all. The fields on either side were a fragrant mass of narcissus flowers, creamy in their unfolding, snow-white when full out. Now and then the white stretches were broken by gleaming globe flowers, big and round and the colour of buttercups. The scent was enough to make anyone go to sleep and dream sweet dreams. Dani was quite drowsy when they reached the outskirts of the village.

But long before they reached the marketplace he was fully awakened by the clamour of cowbells, the lowing of frightened cattle, the shouting of men, and the shrill screams of excited children. When they turned the corner by the fountain and jerked down the shallow steps, bumpety-bump, a scene of wild confusion met their eyes.

The market was a solid mass of cows and calves standing with their flanks pressed against each other. Some were chestnut and some were fawn and white, but they all wore clanging bells and tossed their heads nervously. Here and there cows broke loose. Over by the grocer's shop a crowd of men were shouting at a young bullock that was determined to put his horns through the shop window. And in and out among their legs swarmed the children, for this was a great holiday: school was closed.

For when the grass began to grow long in the fields, the cows went up the mountain for the summer to feed in the high pastures while the hay ripened in the valleys. The farmers went up and lived with them, while the women and children stayed behind. But on the day when the *troupeaux* set out, all the cows assembled before starting on their various routes. Then the children followed their property up to the heights and spent the day in the mountains, settling the cows into their new quarters.

Dani's arrival caused quite a stir, for except for his journey to hospital, this was his first public appearance in the village. Everyone wanted to look at him. All the children wanted to pull his cart. What with the cows and the crowds and the cobbles it was a wonder he wasn't tipped right out. All the women wanted to kiss him too. But Dani wanted to see the *troupeau* and found that kissing hid the view. So he held out his hand firmly and let them kiss that instead of his cheek.

Time was getting on, and the processions must be moving. The farmers were drawing their leader cows out of the crowd. Each *troupeau* shoved its way out after them, for every *troupeau* had its leader who wore a bigger bell than the rest.

Monsieur Burnier was drawing out his leader by the collar, and his cows were making their way out from the mass as best they might. The Burnier leader was one of Paquerette's daughters, a large fawn and white cow, who was called Eglantine. Behind her came a bull calf with a pink nose and shaky legs. This was Paquerette's latest grandson, Napoleon.

Monsieur Burnier walked up to Dani's cart with his hand on the cow's neck.

"The mule cart is waiting round the back of the cobbler's shop," he said, "so put Dani into it, leave the wood cart behind the infant school, and we will start. I will go in front as the mule will soon catch us up."

He went off, rounded up his *troupeau,* and set off up the steep steps behind the clock tower. He looked like a Pied Piper with a stream of children pattering after him, for all the children liked Monsieur Burnier. Very soon the mule, who thought he was going home and was therefore in a hurry, caught them up. Annette was holding the reins and clicking her tongue and Dani was in the back, shouting at the top of his voice.

Dani never forgot that ride up the mountain. Never had there dawned a fresher, sweeter morning, with a sky like sapphire, and a scented wind sweeping over the narcissi. Further up they entered the forest, its dim silence shattered by the pealing bells as the cows plunged up the path, slipping a little on the pine needles. Here Eglantine's little bull calf grew tired and lagged behind. So Dani leaned over and put his hand on his collar and drew him along beside the mule cart.

His father looked back and smiled. "He's tired, poor little thing," he said. "You'd better take him in the cart with you, Dani."

He lifted the wobbly legged creature into the cart, and Dani flung his arms round his woolly neck and shrieked for joy. It was a beautiful calf, with meek eyes, lazy ears, and pale stubby curls on its forehead. So they sat watching the forest together, sniffing the scent of pink daphne bushes and the sap of pine trees.

By the time they came out of the forest they had climbed so high that they could see right over the green mountains that walled in the valley to the snow capped ranges beyond. Here the snows were eternal and never melted. Dani lay back, counting the white peaks, and imagined himself in heaven. He thought surely heaven must be rather like this – lying far above the world, with the music of cowbells clanging round. Then, as though to add the last drop to his cup of happiness, Annette suddenly produced a long twisty roll and a hunk of cheese. She told him to sit up for his dinner. So he sat nibbling one end of the hard golden crust, as the bull calf slept, his warm body pressed against Dani's own.

Annette had left the mule to make his own way and was wandering up and down the slopes picking the alpine flowers that grew in the high pastures, as a present for Grandmother. There were clumps of big anemones, smoky blue and furry on the outside and pure white inside. There were gentians (of an indescribable blue), shaped like bells, and tiny starry gentians that lay flat against the ground. It did occur to Dani that it would be nice to run up and down the slopes to pick flowers with Annette, but he did not think about it for long. There was so much else to be happy about, and, besides, if he had not been lame he would never have had his bear crutches; nor would he have been sitting in the cart with his arms round the bull calf.

The path turned a hairpin bend round the roots of a great battered pine whose branches on one side had been broken off by storms and the weight of the snow. As they turned the corner they came in sight of their summer home – a little shut up cow barn with one living room attached. It was standing in the middle of a meadow of yellow globe flowers. Just behind it rose the last steep slope of the rest of the mountain.

It had a welcoming air, this hut, as though it were longing to be opened up and lived in again. The cows moved a little faster at the sight of it, and their bells pealed out briskly in honour of the homecoming.

A fountain splashed into a wooden trough outside the chalet, and the thirsty cattle plunged their heads into it and enjoyed a long noisy drink. Dani and the calf tumbled out of the cart and the calf drank, too. Then Monsieur Burnier went to the door, turned the key in the lock and went in.

The little chalet was dank and cold after being buried in snow all the winter, but they had brought logs and provisions in the mule cart and they soon had a fire lit. As Annette flung back the shutters the sun came streaming in, showing up the dust everywhere.

Annette went round with broom and duster, and Dani came hopping behind like a cheerful cricket. Monsieur Burnier vanished up a ladder into the loft to bring down armfuls of musty hay for the cows' bedding. Then it was milking time and the cattle wandered in one by one. After that, it was supper time and Monsieur Burnier and Annette sat on stools at the table. Dani sat on the mule rug on the floor because the condition of his leg made stools uncomfortable. They ate bread, smoked sausage and cheese, and drank hot coffee out of enormous wooden bowls. They ate silently because they were tired, and because the brightness of the sun at evening in the Alps was too vivid for speech. It changed everything with a sort of golden glory.

When he had finished his last mouthful, Dani struggled to his feet and held up his arms to his father.

"Do you want to go to bed now?" asked Monsieur Burnier, picking him up.

"No," replied Dani firmly, "I want you to carry me to the top of the mountain!"

Monsieur Burnier looked aghast. The top of the mountain was a good 25 minutes' steep climb, and Dani was a sturdy child. But he always found it impossible to refuse his little son anything. So he burst into a hearty roar of laughter at his own foolishness and started off with Dani on his shoulder, with Annette following behind.

The crest was strewn everywhere with rare, beautiful flowers. Annette ran about among them while Monsieur Burnier strode on, too out of breath to speak. Only when at last they reached the top did he put Dani down, and then they all sat looking about them, and thinking their own thoughts.

For everywhere they looked, blushing snow peaks rose out of a purple sea. The sun was setting, and while twilight had fallen on the valleys the high mountains caught the last rays and were bathed in a bright pink glow. It looked almost as if the Alps were on fire. As they sat watching, the sun sank a little lower until only the very tips still burned crimson. Then the glow faded altogether and there was nothing to be seen at all but cold ice blue mountains with the stars coming out behind them. Soon the moon would rise and then the peaks would turn to cool silver.

Annette sighed and rose to her feet. She hated that cold moment, when the last gleam of light and warmth faded from the mountains. The approach of twilight always made her feel sad and lonely as though she had lost something beautiful for ever. It was a little bit like the night when she woke in the dark and was told that her mother had died.

It was nice to get back to the chalet and see the firelight flickering in the window, and to gather round the blazing logs and shut out the night. The door into the stable was open. The calf came straying in and sat down on the floor by Dani, with its long legs crumpled up underneath it.

"I want to sleep with the calf," announced Dani in his firmest voice.

"No, Dani," said Annette hastily, "you'll catch fleas."

"But if Napoleon had fleas I'd have caught them already in the cart," said Dani. "Please, Papa, I want very badly to sleep with Napoleon!"

Monsieur Burnier smiled and remarked that he thought it could be managed for a treat. So he rigged up a hay mattress covered with a sack. Soon Dani was tucked up on it under the mule rug while Napoleon, triumphant, lay on a heap of straw beside him. Annette, highly disapproving, slept in the one and only bed, and Monsieur Burnier went off and made himself comfortable in the hay loft.

Outside, the moon rose over the mountains and the peaks turned dazzling silver.

12

Lucien did not go up the mountain with his cows, for the Morels possessed only three cows, which they farmed out with another herd for the summer. So until haymaking started in the fields around his home, Lucien had plenty of time after school and visited the old man of the mountain nearly every day.

His horse was nearly finished, and a beautiful little bit of work it was for a boy of Lucien's age. It was a larger figure than he had attempted before, with a flying mane and little hooves that hardly seemed to touch the ground. As he looked at it he thought of speed and slender grace. Lucien spent hours over it, and studied every horse in the neighbourhood so that he might perfect each muscle.

He still had plenty of time because the competition was not to be judged till the end of the haymaking holiday. But already the schoolchildren were beginning to make guesses about the results.

Most of the boys backed Pierre, the postman's son, who was carving a wooden inkstand with two bears standing over the inkwell. He was working hard, and it was a good piece of carving. But Lucien thought the bear could easily have been mistaken for a dog or any other animal. He looked at it silently, while the other children were loud in their admiration.

Nobody could mistake his horse, thought Lucien. It was a horse and nothing but a horse. But no one suspected that he might win the prize, because no one except the master knew he had entered for it. He had been too shy to tell them, too afraid of their scornful faces and their lack of interest. But now, looking at Pierre's bear, he knew that he would win. There was not another entry to touch his. And he saw himself walking up for the prize, and every eye turned on him in admiration and astonishment. They would all be interested and want to see his horse. And then perhaps they would like him better. His face flushed a little at the thought.

There was more discussion about the girls' entries. Marcelle from the shop made beautiful lace, and had done so since she was a very little girl. Jeanne's mother was a dressmaker and she had been brought up in the trade. But Annette was a skilled knitter. Grandmother had taught her when she didn't go to school. Annette had sat on her small stool keeping an eye on Dani and clicking away at her needles, with Grandmother sitting in her armchair ready to give advice when needed.

So Annette was entering a dark blue jersey she had knitted for Dani to wear on Sundays and festivals. It had alpine flowers knitted in bright colours round the neck and waist. She had not yet finished it, but it was a promising article, and everybody praised it as she sat working away in the playground.

"I think you are sure to get the prize, Annette," said several of her friends. "It is harder to do a pattern like that than to make lace like Marcelle. Everyone says so."

Annette was hopeful, too. She wanted so badly to win that prize. It would make up a little for getting such disgracefully low arithmetic marks. And how pleased and proud Grandmother, Father and Dani would be!

However, unlike Lucien, she had very little time, for her after-school hours were always busy. And now the haymaking holidays had begun, and all children worked in the fields from dawn to dusk, side by side with their elders.

A good deal of friendly arranging had to be done at haymaking time. A neighbour who had grown-up sons to help on his farm went up to the high pastures to look after the Burnier cows, while Monsieur Burnier came down to cut the hay on his own slopes. After he had finished, he always went over and cut the hay in the little meadow that belonged to the Morels, because Madame Morel was a widow, and Lucien not yet old enough to wield a scythe. For there were no tractors or mowers on those steep mountain slopes, only great sweeping scythes that mowed the grass in curved swathes all up and down the field. Every swathe was a heap of flowers – purple cranesbills, moon daisies, red sorrels and dark aconites. And behind the man with the scythe came the women and children with wooden rakes, collecting the swathes into tidy heaps. The tiny children had tiny rakes, for no one who was steady on their legs was considered too young to help with the haymaking.

Father and Annette had to work hard, for they had a broad expanse of sloping pasture, and could not afford hired labour. They rose with the sun, in the clear cool dawning when the dew hung heavy on the flowers, and the cocks crowed in the valley. Later on in the day, Grandmother and Dani joined them. Grandmother worked slowly and painfully, and Dani did no work at all, because he could not wield a rake and a crutch at the same time. Instead he kangarooed among the swathes, or buried himself under the haycocks. When he was tired he lay flat on his back in the sun and fell asleep to the song of the scythe.

Monsieur Burnier cut his own meadow first, and then went off to cut the Morel patch, leaving his family to gather in his own swathes. Madame Morel had been a little nervous this year, in case by way of revenge he should refuse to come. But she need not have worried. She woke one morning and from her window saw him hard at work, his body stripped to the waist swinging in rhythm with the scythe.

"Hurry, Lucien," she called, "Monsieur Burnier is already mowing in the meadow. Run out and start on the haycocks."

Lucien shuffled sheepishly into the field and muttered "Good morning!" to Monsieur Burnier, his eyes on the ground. He hated having to work with the man he had wronged and kept as far away from him as possible. Monsieur Burnier had no wish to hold any conversation. It was one thing to mow a neighbour's meadow, but quite another to chat with the boy who had hurt his little son.

Annette arrived at noon with her father's dinner done up in a handkerchief. She also took no notice of Lucien, and when he saw her coming he slunk away into the house.

It took Monsieur Burnier three days to mow the Morel meadow, and the third day was the last day of the holidays. Lucien and his mother and sister were working hard to clear the field before Lucien went back to school. They were all in the meadow when Annette appeared as usual with her bundle and gave it to her father. She was in a hurry, for the next day the children had to give in their entries for the handcraft competition, and Annette still had the finishing touches to put on her jersey.

"I do wonder if I shall get that prize," said Annette to herself. "I do want it so. But even if I don't, Dani will look sweet in the jersey."

The meadow lay at the back, and on her way home Annette passed the front of the house. It was a very hot day, and Annette was thirsty. The door leading from the little veranda into the kitchen stood invitingly open.

I will go in and have a drink from that tap, thought Annette, climbing the veranda steps. She thought there would be no harm in that. Before the accident, she had run in and out of the Morel kitchen as though it were her own.

Having reached the top of the steps, she suddenly stopped dead and stood quite still, staring.

There was a little table set against the outer side of the balcony, with some carving tools and chips of wood on it. And amidst the chips was the figure of a little horse at full gallop, with waving mane and delicate hooves.

Annette stood for a full five minutes gazing at the little creature, lost in thought. Of course it was Lucien's entry for the competition. The deceitful boy had never even told anyone he was submitting an entry, or that he knew how to carve at all.

It was almost perfect. Even Annette's jealous eyes could see that. If Lucien gave it in, he would win the prize easily. No one else could touch him.

And when he won the prize, everybody would begin to admire his work and perhaps they would begin to like him for it. Perhaps they would begin to forget that he had hurt Dani.

Also, if Lucien won the prize he would be happy. He would walk up to receive it with his head in the air. To see Lucien looking happy would be more than Annette could bear. Why should he be happy? He deserved never to be happy again. He would not be happy if she could help it. She had arrived just at a fortunate moment.

The table stood at a level with the veranda railings, and a gust of wind fluttered the shavings of wood. A rather stronger gust of wind could easily blow the light little model over. No one would ever suspect anything else when they found the little horse smashed and trampled below.

Annette put out her hand and pushed it over. It fell on to the stones with a little crack and Annette bounded down the steps and stamped on it. Anyone could accidentally tread on something that had blown over the veranda railings.

So Lucien's horse lay in splinters among the cobbles, and Annette walked slowly home.

But somehow the brightness had gone out of the day, and the world no longer looked quite as beautiful as before. Annette wondered why, for no cloud had passed in front of the sun.

It was not long before she came in sight of her own chalet. As she turned the corner, Dani saw her and gave a loud welcoming shout. Something very, very exciting had happened, and if he had been an ordinary little boy he would have raced to meet her. But, being Dani, he merely came hobbling up the hill as fast as he could, doing enormous leaps on his crutches.

"Nette, Nette," shouted Dani, his eyes shining, "I think there's been some fairies in the woodpile! I made a little house down behind the logs, and I found a tiny little elephant with a long trunk. And then I looked again and I found a camel with a hump, and a rabbit with long ears. And cows and goats and tigers and a giraffe with ever such a long neck. Oh, Nette, come and look at them! They are so beautiful. And no one but the fairies could have put them down behind the woodpile, could they?"

"I don't know," answered Annette, and her voice sounded quite cross. Dani looked up at her in astonishment. She didn't seem a bit pleased at his news, and it was almost the most wonderful thing that had happened to him since he had found Klaus in his slipper on Christmas morning.

However, he thought, when she saw them she was sure to be pleased. She didn't yet know how beautiful they were. He hopped valiantly along, rather out of breath, because Annette was walking faster than she usually did when he was beside her.

He dragged her to the woodpile, and dived behind it, reappearing with the procession of carved animals, arranged on a flat log. He looked anxiously at her, but to his great disappointment there was no sign of surprise or pleasure in her face.

"I expect some other child dropped them, Dani," she said crossly, "and anyhow, it's nothing to make such a fuss about. They're not all that wonderful. And you're too big to believe in fairies."

She turned away and went up the steps, hating herself. She had been unkind to Dani, and spoiled all his happiness. How could she have spoken to him like that? What had happened to her?

But deep down inside her she knew quite well what had happened to her. She had done a mean, deceitful action, and her heart was heavy and dark at the thought of it. All the light and joy seemed to have gone out of life.

And now she could never get rid of it or undo it. She ran upstairs to her bedroom and, flinging herself on the bed, she burst into tears.

13

Lucien ran home from the hay fields with a light heart that evening. He had worked hard, and his body was tired, but his little horse was waiting for him. Tomorrow he would carry it to school and everyone would know that he could carve.

Up the steps he bounded, and then stopped dead. His horse had gone. Only the tools and the chips lay on the table.

Perhaps his mother, who had come home earlier, had taken it in. He hurled himself into the house.

"Mother! Mother!" he cried. "Where have you put my little horse?"

His mother looked up from the soup pot. "I haven't seen it," she replied. "You must have put it somewhere yourself."

Lucien began to get seriously alarmed.

"I haven't," he answered. "I left it on the table, I know I did. Oh, Mother, where can it be? Please help me find it!"

His mother followed him at once. She was just as keen on Lucien's winning the prize as he was himself, and together they hunted high and low. Then Madame Morel had an idea.

"Perhaps it has fallen over the railings, Lucien," she said. "Go and search down below."

So Lucien went down, and searched, but he did not search for long. He found it all too quickly – the scattered splinters that had once been his horse.

He gathered them up in his hand and took them to his mother. Her cry of disappointment brought Marie running, and both of them stood gazing in dismay.

"It must have been the cat," said Marie at last. "I am sorry, Lucien. Haven't you anything else you could take?"

His mother said nothing except "Oh, Lucien!" But the voice in which she said it held more emotion than her son could bear. He said nothing at all. He just went indoors and looked at the clock on the wall.

"I'm going up the mountain," he said, in a voice that tried hard to be steady. "I won't be home for supper."

He ran down the steps and up through the hay field where the swathes lay like waves in a green sea. His mother watched him with a troubled face until he disappeared into the forest. Then she went back inside and wept a few tears into the soup pot.

"Everything goes wrong for that boy," she murmured sadly. "Will he never succeed in anything?"

Lucien trudged through the forest, seeing nothing. Little grey squirrels leaped from branch to branch and flung acorns at each other, but he took no notice of them. He could think of nothing at all but his lost prize and his bitter disappointment – how someone else would get the honour that he deserved. He would continue to be disliked and despised. He would never get another chance to show the others how good he was at carving. No one would be interested unless he had won that prize.

He had reached a clearing in the forest, and he could see over the treetops to the ranges of white peaks beyond the mountains that shut in his immediate valley.

I wish I could go right away, he thought to himself, and start all over again where nobody knew me, or knew what I'd done. If I could go and live in another valley, I shouldn't feel afraid of everybody as I am here.

His eyes rested on the Pass that ran between two opposite peaks and led to the big town in the next valley where Marie worked. The sight of that Pass always fascinated him. It seemed like a road leading into a world beyond, away from all that was safe and familiar – an eerie spot where daring travellers had been caught in blizzards and perished in the waste. He had never crossed it himself, but had heard that in summer when the sun was shining, the Pass was strewn with flowers. Now it was bright with the last rays. To Lucien's gaze it suddenly seemed like a door of escape from some prison; a door he must pass through alone, to find release in a land of sunset.

Before he realised it, he was drawing close to the old man's little home. The old man was sitting at his front door, his chin resting on his hands, gazing intently at the mountains on the other side of the valley. Not till the boy was quite close to him did he look up.

"Ah," said the old man in his deep mumbling voice, "it is you again. Well, how goes the carving, and when are you going to win that prize?"

"I am not going to win the prize," replied Lucien sullenly. "My horse is smashed to pieces. I think the cat knocked it over the railings, and someone trampled on it."

"I am sorry," said the old man gently, "but surely you can enter something else! What about that chamois you carved? That was a good piece of work for a boy."

Lucien kicked at the stones on the path savagely.

"I did it without proper tools," he muttered, "and they would think it was my best work. No, if I cannot enter my little horse, I will enter nothing."

"But does it matter what they think?" asked the old man.

"Yes."

"Why?"

Lucien stared at the ground. What could he answer to that? But the old man was his friend… the only friend he had. Maybe he had better try to speak the truth.

"It matters very much," he said, "because they all hate me and think me stupid and bad. If I won a prize, and they saw I could carve better than any other boy in the valley, they might like me better."

"They wouldn't," the old man said simply. "Your skill when used for your own ends will never buy you love. It may buy you admiration and envy, but never love. If that was what you were after, you have wasted your time."

Lucien continued to stare at the ground. Then suddenly he looked up into the old man's face, his eyes brimming with tears.

"Then it is all no good," he whispered haltingly. "There seems no way to start again, and to make them like me. I suppose they just never will."

"If you want them to like you," replied the old man steadily, "you must make yourself fit to be liked. You must use your skill in loving and serving them. It will not happen all at once. It may even take years. But you must persevere."

Lucien stared at the old man. There was an unspoken question on his lips. This strange old man, who seemed to know so much about the way of love, why did he shut himself away up here, cut off from other people?

The old man seemed to guess the boy's thoughts. Perhaps the puzzled frown on Lucien's forehead and the way he stared gave his thoughts away.

"You wonder why I should talk of loving and serving others, do you?" said the old man. "You were right to wonder such a thing. It is a long story, too."

"Well," admitted Lucien, "I was thinking that it must be difficult to love and serve people when you live alone up here and never speak to anyone but me."

The old man sat silent for some moments, looking out over the far rocky peaks which the sunset was touching with gold. Then he said, "I will tell you my story, but remember, it is a secret. I have never told it to another living soul. But you have trusted me, and I will trust you, too."

Lucien flushed. Those were good words. Even the prize and his disappointment seemed to matter less. It was better to be trusted than to win prizes.

"I will start at the beginning," said the old man simply. "I was an only child, and there was nothing in the world my father would not give me. If ever a child was spoiled, it was I.

"I was a clever boy, for all my selfishness, and when I grew up I was given a good post in the bank. I worked hard and climbed to the top. I fell in love with a girl, and married her. God gave us two little sons, and for the first few years of our life together I believe I was a good father and a good husband.

"But I got in with a bad lot of friends who flattered me and invited me to their homes. They were interested in gambling, and they drank heavily. I admired them and began to learn their ways. Gradually I began to spend more and more money on drink and gambling.

"I need not tell you much about those years. I was less and less at home, and often came home drunk in the evenings. My little boys grew to fear me and dislike me. My wife pleaded with and prayed for me, but I could not give it up. Drink had me in its grip, and I knew of no power stronger than myself that could free me.

"Our money began to dwindle away, and people began to talk about my bad ways. The bank manager warned me twice, but the third time, when I was found drunk and disorderly in the streets, he dismissed me. That day I went home sober and told my wife I had lost my job. She simply replied, 'Then I shall have to go out and work. We can't fail our boys.'

"I tried to find another job, but my story was known, and no one would employ me. I tried to earn money on the gambling tables, but I never had any luck. I lost the little I had.

"My wife went out daily to work, as well as looking after the house and the boys. But she could not earn enough to keep us all. One day she came and told me we were in debt, and could not pay.

"I was desperate for money, to pay our debts and to buy myself more drink. I had not worked in the bank as a high and trusted official for nothing. I knew the ways of it inside out, and I decided to commit a robbery.

"My plan was a skilful one, but it was not quite skilful enough. I was discovered, and tried. I was condemned to a long term of imprisonment.

"My wife had been ill for many weeks. She was hopelessly overworked, and ate next to nothing so that there should be enough for the boys. Three times she came to the prison to visit me, pale and worn to a shadow. Then my elder boy wrote that she was too ill to come. A few weeks later a policeman escorted me to her bedside to say goodbye to her. She was dying. They say she died of consumption. I say she died of a broken heart, and I killed her.

"I sat beside her for 24 hours, with her hand in mine. She spoke to me about the love and mercy of God, and about the forgiveness of wrongs. I stayed with her until she died, and then they took me back to prison.

"I remember little about the months that followed. I seemed numbed and lost in despair. I had only one comfort. All my life I had loved woodcarving. In my spare hours in the common room they let me have my tools and whittle away at bits of wood. I grew more and more skilful and a kindly warden used to take my work out and sell it in the town. I earned a little money in that way and saved it eagerly. One day I supposed I should have to start again.

"The day came sooner than I expected. I was summoned to the governor and told that I would be released because of my good conduct. In three weeks' time I should be a free man.

"I wandered back to the prisoners' common room hardly knowing whether to be pleased or sorry. I supposed I should be glad to leave prison. But where should I go, and how should I start life again? One thing I had determined. My boys should never see me again, or know where I was. They had been adopted by their grandparents, and I knew they were growing up into fine, intelligent boys with good futures ahead of them. They should never be branded with my bad name or shadowed by my past. To them I would be as though I were dead.

"Beyond that, I knew nothing. The governor offered to help me start again, but I wanted to leave no traces of where I was going, and refused his help. When the day of my release came, I walked out with my little sum of money in my pocket and took the first train up into the mountains.

"I got out at this village, because I saw a man in difficulty with a herd of cows who were trying to push through a broken fence. I helped him get them back into the road, and then asked him if he could give me work.

"He did not need me, but pointed to a chalet, halfway up the mountain. Up there, he told me, was a peasant whose son had gone to the town to learn a trade. He badly needed someone to take the place of his son.

"I shall never forget that day! The narcissus flowers were out in the fields as I climbed the hill. I found the chalet, and the man himself was chopping wood outside when I arrived. I went and stood in front of him. I was tired and hungry and sick at heart, and wasted no time in words.

"'I hear you need a herdsman,' I began. 'Will you take me?'

"He looked me up and down. His face was good and his eyes were kind.

"'You are not from our village,' he said. 'Where have you come from, and who are you?'

"'I come from Geneva,' I said, for that is where I was born.

"'What is your work?'

"'I have none.'

"'But what have you been doing up to now?'

"I cast about in my mind for some good lie, but the man looked at me so straight, and his face was so honest, that the lie died on my lips. I wanted him to know me for what I was, or else not to know me at all.

"'I have just come out of prison,' I replied simply.

"'Why were you in prison?'

"'For stealing money.'

"'How do I know that you will not steal my money?'

"'Because I want to start again, and I am asking you to trust me. If you do not trust me I will go away.'

"Then he held out his hand to me, and I sat down on the bench beside him and wept. Prison makes a man very weak.

"I worked for that man for five years, early and late. I made friends with no one and took no rest. My only joy was to work for this good man who had helped me when everyone else had cast me out. I often wondered why he did it, until one night I heard him talking to his son, who was home from town for the weekend.

"'Father,' said the boy, 'why did you take in that prisoner without any character? Surely it was a very unwise thing to do!'

"'My son,' answered the man. 'Jesus Christ loved those who did wrong and helped them. And we are his disciples.'

"In the summer he and I took the cows up the mountain, and lived in this chalet where I live now. And the peace of the mountain seemed to enter into me and heal me. For me, the bad man, as for him, the good man, the flowers grew on the slopes, the sunsets were beautiful, and the early mornings were cloudless. There was no difference. I, too, began to think about God.

"But my master began to grow weak and ill. He visited the doctor, but nothing could be done for him. I cared for him for a year and his son often came to see him. But at the end of that time he died, and I was left alone. The night before he left this earth he spoke to me, as my wife had done, about the love and mercy of God and about how he would forgive me.

"So I lost my only friend, although his son was very good to me. His son was a rich man by now. He sold the cows and gave me this chalet for my own. So I bought a goat and a few hens, collected my few possessions and came here and have lived here ever since.

"I have only one friend now… except for you, of course, my young companion. The shopkeeper in the town who sells my carvings. He sometimes gives me news of my sons. They have grown up into good men and they have done well. One is a doctor and one is a businessman. They do not know that I am alive, and it is better that way. I have nothing that I could give them, and my name would only disgrace them.

"But through the lives and the words of my master and my wife, I too have come to believe in the love and mercy of God and the forgiveness of wrongs. I cannot pay back the people I robbed, for I don't know who they are, but nevertheless I am working hard. I have now saved nearly as much money as I stole, and when I have saved the whole sum I will seek for some person or some cause who truly needs it. And to them I will pay my debt.

"You say there is no way to start again, but you are wrong. I have done more wrong than you have, and have suffered in a way that a child like you cannot know. But I believe that God has forgiven me. I am spending my days working to give back what I owe to humanity, and striving to become what God meant me to be. It is all I can do. It is all *anyone* can do. The past we must leave to God."

The goat had come up and rested its brown head on the old man's knee. Now it butted at the old man's waistcoat to remind him it was milking time.

"I must go," said Lucien. "But I will remember what you have told me."

He walked home slowly. "I am spending my days working to give back what I owe… striving to become what God meant me to be." He thought about it a lot – so much so that the matter of the prize seemed quite small, and he found that he had stopped minding so very much.

Well, he couldn't restore Dani's leg, but one day he might get the chance to do something great for him. And as for the second part, he could at least try to be a nicer boy. There was his mother, for instance. She was miserable because his carving was broken. Well, he would be brave, and show her he didn't mind, and then she would be happy again.

As he left the wood he could see the orange lights in his chalet windows, warm and welcoming, shining out into the summer dusk. The crickets were chirping in the fields, and the newly cut hay smelt sweet and strong. A baby sickle moon hung poised over the black pines. It was like the old man had said, for Lucien could see that the night was kind to good children and bad children alike.

He ran lightly up the chalet steps and kissed his mother, who was standing on the balcony watching for him.

"I'm hungry, Mother," he said cheerily. "Have you saved my supper?"

And over his bowl of soup he smiled at her, and the shadow passed from her eyes as she smiled back.

14

The sun woke Dani at daybreak next morning, and he lay for a few minutes trying to remember what great event was going to happen that day. It soon came back to him, and he sat up in bed and shouted for Annette.

"Nette," he shouted, "come quick! I'm coming to see you get a prize! Bring me my best black velvet suit and my embroidered braces and my waistcoat. Quick!"

Annette, in her bed which was now placed at the top of the stairs, pretended not to hear at first. Then she sat up.

"Be quiet, Dani," she called back grumpily. "I don't suppose I shall get the prize at all, and anyhow it's much too early to dress. Father's only just got up."

Dani sighed, and lay down again, but he was too excited to stop talking. He pulled Klaus into bed with him and began whispering into one of her shining white ears.

"I shall go in the cart, Klaus," murmured Dani, "and I shall see all the things the children have made. But Annette's is the best, and I shall see her get a lovely prize, and I'll clap as loud as I can. And I shall wear my best braces."

Klaus yawned. So did Dani. After all, it was very early in the morning. And when Annette came down later she found them curled up together, fast asleep.

One and a half hours later they were off. Dani was dressed in his best black velvet suit and embroidered braces. His father pulled the cart, and Annette walked beside him, dull and sad and rather cross.

Dani was puzzled. What could be making Annette dull and sad on such a morning? The sun was shining, the river was glistening, and Annette was going to win a prize. There was everything to make them happy and, anyhow, Dani never felt sad or cross except when he had a pain in his leg.

"Have you got a tummy-ache, Nette?" asked Dani, suddenly.

"Of course I haven't, Dani," answered Annette shortly. "Why should I have a tummy-ache?"

"I just thought you might," explained Dani. "Oh, Nette, look, there's a blue butterfly sitting on my shoe."

But Annette did not even turn round to look at the blue butterfly. She walked on, staring at the ground. Whatever could be the matter with Annette?

Already the schoolroom was filling when they arrived. The desks had been stacked on one side. The children's work was laid out on long tables, and a very pretty show it made. Mothers, fathers, uncles, aunts and grandparents walked round admiringly. The children jostled and nudged each other, pointing and chattering like magpies.

There was the knitting table covered with brightly coloured specimens of the children's work. There was the embroidery table, bright with embroidered aprons and belts. There was the lacemaking table and the crochet table. Then there was the boys' work with specimens of woodwork and carving, all carefully arranged.

Pierre, the postman's son, was standing bright-eyed and confident close to his own piece of work – the wooden inkstand with the bear standing over the inkwell.

Pierre had worked and worked on the carving to make it look more bear-like. And he had done well. The snout was a little crooked, and the bear's flanks were definitely fatter one side than the other. Still, it now definitely looked like a bear and it was a good piece of work for a child of Pierre's age. Pierre, who was a nice boy, blushed a little and looked the other way as his friends slapped him on the back and said "Well done!". Still, he was very pleased with that little bear himself, and he looked up and smiled proudly at his mother who was coming towards him.

Lucien was there too, wandering round by himself as usual, for his mother was busy and had not come down. He stared gloomily at the inkstand and compared that heavy stuck bear with his own sprightly horse. If only that accident had not happened, the children would have been standing round him instead of round Pierre. He felt a great angry stab of jealousy for Pierre, who was clever, good-looking, good at games, and who now was going to win the prize that belonged to him, Lucien. He drifted away into a corner by himself and stared gloomily at the crowd.

Annette, surrounded by a chattering group of friends, was strangely silent. Some thought she would get the prize, some said Marcelle or Jeanne would get it. There was much guessing, much running to and fro, and much putting together of heads, some saying one thing and some another. Only Annette, usually so talkative said nothing.

Dani, his hand clasped tightly in his father's, hopped round inspecting everything, and everyone made way for him and gave him a kind word as he passed. Then, having seen all there was to see, he stood at the end of the long table close to Annette's entry, so that he might be right on the spot when the prize-winner was announced. Being a very small boy, there was nothing to be seen of him above the top of the table but his unruly thatch of sun-bleached hair and his round blue eyes. And they were very wide open and anxious.

The door opened, and a sudden hush fell on the chattering crowd. The inspector, an important man from the town by the lake, had arrived to judge the work. The children and their families stood quietly against the walls as the tall man walked slowly round, picking up and examining first one thing and then another. He praised a great many objects and spoke kindly of all. He had come prepared to see a good exhibition, he said, and he was not disappointed. He looked through the children's exercise books, piled on a table in the far end of the room, and talked about their work. Everyone could see he was a kind, patient man... but very slow. All the children wanted to know was, who was going to get the prize?

Well, he was going to make up his mind about the girls first. He walked over to Marcelle's lace and examined it carefully, and then he went back to Annette's knitted jersey, and stood turning it over in his hands. The room was silent.

Then suddenly the silence was broken.

"My sister made that," said a clear voice.

The big man jumped and peered over the end of the table. He saw a small face lifted to his, full of hope and eagerness. Just for a moment he wondered why he suddenly found himself thinking of a young beech tree bursting into leaf in the sunshine.

"Then your sister is a very clever girl," replied the big man gravely.

"I think it's the very best of all, don't you?" went on Dani earnestly. He did not care that everyone in the room was listening to him. The only thing he cared about was that Annette should win the prize.

As a matter of fact, the big man had already made up his mind when Dani first spoke and he smiled.

"Yes, I do. I think it's the very best," answered the big man. Dani, without any hesitation, turned round on his crutches and faced his sister. She was blushing deeply at his bad behaviour.

"You've got the prize, Nette!" called Dani, and everybody burst out laughing and started clapping.

Pierre won the boys' prize. It was announced properly after a dull speech to which none of the children listened. Then there was tea – rolls and gingerbread and macaroons. Then Pierre went outside with a crowd of admiring friends. They all played leapfrog, and bought chocolate sticks for Pierre by way of congratulation. Then he went home and ate the fruit tart his mother had cooked him for his supper, and was sick in the night.

Lucien went down to the village alone to fetch the loaf. When he came back past the school, the playground was deserted and the children had all gone home. He climbed the hill slowly. But it was not the weight of the breadbasket on his back that bowed his shoulders and made him walk with his eyes on the ground.

Lucien was very unhappy. Why was it that one day it seemed easy to be brave and cheerful, and the next day it seemed impossible to be anything but angry and jealous? Yesterday, on the way home from the old man he had thought that he would not mind seeing Pierre get the prize, but today he hated Pierre. The old man had talked about striving to become what God meant you to be. But somehow, however hard you tried, it seemed impossible to change yourself for long.

And yet the old man had become different, and Lucien found himself wondering how. The old man had talked about God. Perhaps God could make nasty people nice if they asked him. Lucien felt he didn't know very much about God. And anyhow, he thought sadly, God was probably very angry with him for being so horrible to Dani. Surely God could not love him much. Surely God wouldn't forgive a sin like that in a hurry? Even if God did, thought Lucien, nobody else would. His unhappiness came surging back over him. He gave a great sniff, and kicked angrily at the stones on the path.

He was passing the corner where the path divided not far from Annette's chalet. As he branched off towards his own home, his ear was caught by the sound of a little child singing, and he turned to look.

Dani and Klaus were sitting on a hollowed-out pile of new hay, like two birds in a nest. Dani's head was bent low over something, as he happily sang away to himself. His crutches lay on the ground beside him.

Lucien drew a step nearer and stood watching. Suddenly his cheeks flushed with pleasure and he drew a sharp little breath. For Dani had dug out a sort of cave in the wall of his hay nest, and inside it were grouped all the little wooden animals that he, Lucien, had carved with such care.

So Annette *did* give them to him, thought Lucien to himself, with a little thrill of happiness, and he likes them! Aloud he added, "What are you playing with, Dani?"

Dani jumped, and looked up and saw the boy who had tried to kill his kitten. His first reaction was to seize Klaus and say, "Go away!"

But as he said it, he could not help noticing that Lucien looked very unhappy, and unhappiness was a thing that his friendly little heart could not bear. So, still holding the struggling and indignant Klaus very tightly, he added after a moment's pause, "I'm playing with my fairy Noah animals, but Nette said I mustn't talk to you."

"But I wouldn't hurt you," answered Lucien very gently, "and I'm very sorry about your leg. That's why I made those animals for you."

"You didn't make them," answered Dani with a puzzled frown. "I found them in the woodpile. The fairies put them there."

Lucien was just about to answer, when Annette's voice came sharp and shrill from the door of the chalet.

"Dani!" she shouted. "Come in at once! Supper's ready."

Lucien turned away. So she didn't tell him, he thought, rather bitterly. Still, it was nice to know that Dani loved them and played with them. One day he might get a chance to explain, and then perhaps he and Dani would be friends. He climbed the path between the hay fields slightly comforted.

Dani hopped into the kitchen, climbed into his seat, and hugged his empty tummy while his nose twitched like a rabbit's at the smell of Grandmother's potato soup.

"Nette," began Dani, "Lucien said that he made my fairy Noah animals. But he didn't, did he? The fairies put them in the woodpile, didn't they? He wasn't speaking the truth, was he?"

"I've told you not to talk to Lucien, Dani," said Annette crossly. "He'll only hurt you again. He's a horrible boy."

"Yes," answered Dani, "and I only talked to him a teeny, weeny bit. But he didn't make those animals, did he, Nette? Tell me!"

Annette hesitated. She was a truthful child, and she did not want to tell a lie. But if Dani knew, he would be so grateful that he would forgive Lucien at once, and go and thank him. Then there was no telling where it would all end. They might even become good friends! It was hard enough as it was to make Dani be unfriendly with anybody, but if he knew about the animals it would be quite impossible.

"You know you found them in the woodpile," she replied, looking away, "so how could he have made them? Don't be silly, Dani!"

"Well, he said he did," answered Dani, "but I knew he didn't. It must have been the fairies, mustn't it, Nette?"

"Oh, I don't know, Dani," replied Annette wearily. "How you do chatter! Eat your soup up quickly. It will be all cold."

Dani obediently buried his nose in his bowl. But Grandmother, whose dim old eyes saw more than most people's, looked very hard at Annette. She too had heard and wondered at the story of the animals in the woodpile.

Annette, knowing that Grandmother was looking hard at her, went very red. She moved over to the stove and pretended to help herself to some more soup. But she only took a little, for somehow she wasn't hungry. The day she had looked forward to for so long was all spoiled. She had got the prize she wanted so badly, but it hadn't made her a bit happy. In fact, she was miserable.

She washed up the supper things in silence, tucked up and kissed a warm, sleepy Dani, and slipped outside alone. She usually loved being alone on summer evenings – just her and the still blue mountains. She loved to be alone to look at what she wanted, and to think and play what she liked and go where she pleased.

But tonight it was different. The rushing of the river and the chirping of the crickets, even the lazy goat-bells seemed strange, unfriendly sounds. The shadowed fields seemed lonely and frightening. She didn't want to think, because she could think of nothing but that little smashed horse lying trampled on the ground, and of the light that had died in Dani's face when she had spoken so crossly to him.

Perhaps I shall never like being alone again, thought poor Annette, and she turned back towards home. I wish I could tell someone! It wouldn't be so bad then. I wish my mother was still alive. Oh, I wish, I wish, I wish I hadn't done it!

15

The summer lengthened into autumn, the cows came home down the mountain, and the second mowings were gathered in. Then Annette pulled Dani in his cart up to the nut bushes, and they gathered baskets full of hazel nuts. Dani was growing taller every day, and by October the village cobbler had to make him a new pair of boots. He went to the infant school, too, every day, and Monsieur Burnier paid two big boys one franc each a week to pull him home in the cart.

And now Christmas had come round again. The snow lay deep on the chalet roofs, and Father had had to dig a path from the front door to the main sledge track. The river was silent and frozen, a tiny trickle muffled by the snow on the boulders, while icicles hung like bright swords from the rocks. Annette and Dani went to school on the sledge every morning by starlight, but came home in the sunshine under a deep blue sky, the snow sparkling like jewels.

Christmas was a very special time to Dani, for all the great events of his life had happened at Christmas. His mother had died on Christmas Eve. Although Dani had never known and missed his mother, yet even he sensed a certain gentle sadness in his father's face. Dani himself had had all the mothering he needed from Grandmother and Annette. The only time he ever thought about his mother was when Grandmother read about heaven in the Bible. Then he would gaze up at the photograph on the wall, and think that when he went there, it would be nice to see that kind face looking out for him and smiling to welcome him.

It was his own birthday, too, and this year he was 6. He had thought for a long time about being 6, and he expected to wake up quite a new child on the morning of Christmas Eve. So it was a little disappointing to find, as he lay in the warm shuttered darkness, that he really felt no bigger, or stronger than the day before. Then he remembered that he was going to see the Christmas tree in the church, and Grandmother had made a special cake for his birthday. After that, there was no room for disappointed thoughts any longer.

And of course, according to Dani, Christmas was Klaus' birthday, too. It wasn't really Klaus' birthday, because Klaus must have been at least a fortnight old when she crept into Dani's slipper. But Dani had never thought of that. For him Klaus had begun early Christmas morning, straight from a reindeer sledge, a white ball of Christmas magic, born of stars and snow. So Annette bought some red ribbon at the village shop, and Klaus went about over the Christmas season with a large bow on her neck. She looked very handsome but uncomfortable and scratched anyone who paid any attention to her.

Best of all, it was the birthday of the Lord Jesus. Although Dani did not talk about it very much, he thought about it a lot. It made him strangely happy to know that he shared the birthday of God's own Son.

"What could I give to the Lord Jesus for a birthday present?" he had asked, resting his elbows on Grandmother's knee, and looking up into her face.

"You can give your own self to him," Grandmother had answered, pausing a moment in her knitting. "And you can ask him to make you very loving and able to do what he would like you to do. That will please him better than anything."

So throughout Christmas, Dani tried to be loving and obedient, in order to please God's Son, whose birthday he shared. His love just overflowed to everyone. He tidied Grandmother's workbox, and wiped the dishes for Annette. In the afternoon, he went out to the shed and visited the cows in turn, and told them "Happy Christmas." And at the end of the day, when he knelt to pray, he whispered, "I hope I am giving you a happy birthday, Lord Jesus."

When evening came and it was time to wrap up and go down to the church, Dani was so happy that he felt he might burst.

To begin with, there was the ride on the sledge sandwiched between Father and Annette, with the air so cold he couldn't feel his nose. It was almost full moon, and the white mountains looked quite silver. All the trees in the forest were weighed down with snow, and the lower branches trembled as they rushed past, powdering Dani's little hood. The smooth firm sound of the sledge runners cutting along the track was thrilling music. And the clasp of Annette's arms round his middle was warm and reassuring to a little boy out at night in such a strange silver world.

Out of the wood, over the bumpy little bridge they went, and on down across the last field with a cold rush. Then they saw the little church with the rosy light of hundreds of candles streaming from the windows and door, and the muffled forms of the villagers greeting each other in the porch.

Dani was carried up the aisle in Father's arms and placed on the front bench with the other children from the infant school – 30 rosy-faced children in woolly hoods gazing open-mouthed at the tree. Only three days ago it had been weighed down with snow in the cold forest near

Dani's home. Now it was jewelled and decked and glistening, festooned with oranges, chocolate sticks and shining gingerbread bears.

Dani was glad he was sitting in front, partly because he could see the tree, and partly because he could see "his" picture. It hung behind the pulpit – a great big picture of the Good Samaritan. It was hung in a wooden frame, and had been drawn by a famous Swiss artist. Dani loved the kind face of the Good Samaritan, and he loved the little donkey. But best of all he loved the big St Bernard dog who tripped along beside them. It was exactly like Rudolf, the St Bernard dog who pulled the milk cart round the market square. He actually belonged to the milkman, but all the babies in the village thought he belonged to them. They flung their fat arms round his neck, and he was patient with them and treated them as though they were a crowd of naughty puppies. That was why every toddler in the village loved to come to church and see the picture of the Good Samaritan, with Rudolf trotting beside him.

The older schoolchildren sang a carol first. It was a sweet, sad song, supposed to be Mary singing to the sleeping child on her knee.

Dormez, dormez sur mes genoux;
O, petit Jésus, endormez-vous!

Annette was singing it with the others, and her thoughts flew back to that Christmas night when she had first held Dani in her arms. How they had welcomed him and watched him. Yet Jesus was not welcomed by everyone – they "laid him in a bed of hay, because there was no room for them in the inn."

The carol finished, the older children went back to their seats and the infant school trotted to the front. Dani got left behind because crutches did not move as fast as sturdy legs encased in woollen stockings and boots. But they waited for him, and everyone in the audience smiled as he reached his place with a final hop and turned to grin at them.

Voici Noël,
O douce nuit!
L'étoile est là
Qui nous conduit.

Dani glanced up at the bright star on top of the Christmas tree and saw it reflected on the shining gingerbread bears below. He forgot what he was singing because he was wondering which particular bear was going to belong to him. There was one which looked as if it was laughing at the Christmas star. The baker had accidentally given a little twist to its snout. Dani thought he would like that one, and laughed back at it.

As the babies strayed to their seats with backward looks at the tree, the old pastor climbed into the pulpit. He had been pastor in that village for 45 years and everybody loved him. His shoulders were bowed and his skin tanned, for he still climbed the mountains in all weathers to visit his scattered flock, the people under his care. He had a long, white beard. So Dani, with his head full of the tree, got him mixed up in his mind with Father Christmas, and wondered why he was wearing a black coat instead of a red one.

Now the pastor looked down on the people that he loved. He was a very old man, so he knew this might be his last Christmas message. He prayed that he might speak words that would not be forgotten.

Annette listened rather dreamily to the story she knew so well, half thinking of other things. Then the old man suddenly repeated the words that had haunted her every Christmas since the night when she had imagined herself as Jesus' mother Mary, with all doors shut against her.

"'…there was no room for them…' No room for him.

In the unhurried manner of very old people, he repeated it three times, and each time Annette thought the words sounded sadder. How quickly she would have opened her door!

"And yet," went on the old man, "tonight the Saviour is still standing at closed doors. There are still hearts that have never made room for him. This is what he says: 'Listen! I am standing and knocking at your door. If you hear my voice and open the door, I will come in'.

"What will you do about him this Christmas? Will you open the door, or will you leave him standing outside? Will those sad words be said about you, 'There was no room for him'?"

I should like to ask him to come in, thought Annette, I wonder what it all means. The pastor spoke about asking him to come into our hearts. I wonder if I could ask him into *my* heart.

Just for a moment Annette thought it rather a nice idea, and looked round to see whether other people thought it was, too. And as she looked round she suddenly noticed Lucien sitting on the other side of the church, with his mother and sister.

And as she caught sight of him she realised that she couldn't ask the Saviour to come into her heart because her heart was so full of hatred for Lucien. And, of course, the Saviour would not want to come into an angry, unforgiving heart. Either she would have to forgive and be kind, or else the Lord Jesus would have to stay outside.

And she didn't want to forgive and be kind. Not yet.

There was something else, too. She had broken Lucien's carving. She knew he thought it was the cat. She'd heard his mother saying something about it to Marie. And Annette had *let* him think it was the cat. She had cheated him of his prize. If the Lord Jesus came into her heart, he would have something to say to her about that, and she did not want to listen.

The sermon was over, but she had not heard much of it because she had been so busy with her thoughts. So busy that she almost forgot it was time for Dani to go up and get his bear. He had to come and remind her.

The church was full of a low murmur of conversation, and the little ones were surging forward to the tree. Monsieur Pilet, the woodcutter, was giving out the bears. Dani gave his sleeve a firm tug and pointed to the top bear who was laughing at the Christmas star.

"Please, I want that one," he whispered, "that one up there. Please, I want it very badly!"

Because he felt sorry for Dani, and because it was Christmas, Monsieur Pilet moved the ladders, moved the children, and moved the lower lights. Then, with immense difficulty and inconvenience, he climbed up and took hold of the bear that Dani wanted. And Dani went home through the starlight and the snow with the bear of his choice held close to him. Every time he looked down at that merry curved snout he chuckled, as though he and his bear had some private Christmas joke between them that nobody else knew about.

16

Christmas Day was over, and Dani was asleep with his flushed cheek pillowed on his arm. Father was across in the stable, and Annette and Grandmother sat one each side of the stove. Grandmother was knitting white woollen stockings for her grandchildren, and Annette was supposed to be patching her pinafore. But actually her pinafore had slipped to the ground and she was simply staring in front of her with her chin resting on her hands.

"Annette," said Grandmother, without looking up from her knitting, "have you had a happy Christmas?"

"Yes, thank you, Grandma," replied Annette rather dully, because that was what she supposed she ought to say. And then she added suddenly, "Grandma, what does it mean when it says that Jesus knocks at the door of our hearts?"

"It means," said Grandmother, laying down her knitting, and giving Annette her whole attention, "that the Saviour sees that your life is full of wrong things and dark thoughts. He came down and was crucified so that he might take the punishment of those wrong deeds and those dark thoughts instead of you. Then he came to life again so that he could come into your heart and live in you by his Holy Spirit. He can turn out all those wrong thoughts, and think his good, loving thoughts in you instead. It is like a man knocking at the door of a dirty, dark, dusty house, and saying, 'If you will let me in, I will take away the dust and the darkness and make it beautiful and bright.' But, remember, he never pushes in. He only asks if he may come in. That is what knocking means. You have to say, 'Yes, Lord Jesus, I need you and I want you to come and live in me.' *That* is what opening the door means."

Annette's eyes were fixed on Grandmother. There was a long, long pause.

Annette broke the silence.

"But Grandma," she said, drawing her stool nearer and leaning against the old woman's knee, "if you hated someone you could not ask Jesus to come in, could you?"

"If you hate someone," said Grandmother, "it just shows how badly you need to ask him to come in. The darker the room, the more it needs the light."

"But I could never stop hating Lucien," said Annette softly, fingering her long plaits thoughtfully.

"No," said Grandmother. "You're quite right. None of us can stop ourselves thinking wrong thoughts, and it isn't much good trying. But Annette, think about when you come down in the morning and find this room dark with the shutters closed. Do you say to yourself, 'I must chase away the darkness and the shadows first, and then I will open the shutters and let in the sun'? Do you waste time trying to get rid of the dark?"

"Of course not!" said Annette.

"Then how do you get rid of the dark?"

"Well, I pull back the shutters, of course, and then the light comes in!"

"But what happens to the dark?"

"I don't know. It just goes when the light comes!"

"That is just what happens when you ask the Lord Jesus to come in," said Grandmother. "He is love. When love comes in, hatred and selfishness and unkindness will give way to it, just as the darkness gives way when you let in the sunshine. But to try to chase it out alone would be like trying to chase the shadows out of a dark room. It would be a waste of time."

Annette did not answer. Only she sat for a little time staring at the wall, and then she picked up her pinafore with a sigh and worked at it in silence. After a while she got up, kissed her grandmother goodnight very quietly, and went to bed.

But she could not go to sleep for a long time. She lay in the dark, tossing and turning and wondering.

"It's quite true," she said to herself. "If I asked him to come in, I should have to be friends with Lucien, and I don't want to be. And I suppose I should have to tell how I broke his carving, and I could never, never do that. I shall just have to try to forget about the knocking. Yet I feel so terribly miserable."

She did not know yet that if someone hears the Lord Jesus knocking and shuts him out, they are also shutting out happiness. She thought that she could forget all about it and find some other way of being happy. So she turned her hot pillow over, and made herself count the goats running to pasture until she fell asleep.

But in her sleep she dreamed of a dark house with no welcome lights in the windows, and the door barred and bolted. Somebody came to it at night across the waste of snow, and she could see his footprints all the way. This visitor knocked at the door, slowly and patiently, but nobody came to open it. He felt for a handle, but there wasn't one. The wind blew and the clouds raced across the moon, but he didn't go away. He went on knocking and knocking and knocking. He went on knocking until Annette woke up. But still nobody answered and there were still no lights in the windows.

Perhaps there's nobody there, thought Annette to herself in a half-asleep sort of way. But somehow she knew perfectly well that there was. Only they just didn't want to come to the door.

The sadness of the dream stayed with her. She dressed and went down to breakfast rather miserable, only to find everything in a turmoil, because Dani had lost Klaus. He was refusing to eat his breakfast until she was found.

"She always wakes me in the morning," said Dani, worried. "She comes and purrs at me. But this morning she wasn't there. She went out last night before I went to sleep and she hasn't come back."

Dani's distress was terrible to behold and the whole household was moved. Father did an outside tour of the barns, Grandmother rummaged about in the kitchen, and Dani explored impossible places. Annette went upstairs and searched the bedrooms, but it was all in vain. Klaus was nowhere to be found. Father had last seen her stalking towards the barn with her tail in the air, picking her way gingerly across the soft snow. No one had seen her since.

It was a wretched day. Dani broke down at dinner, and between his sobs declared that he could not eat anything because Klaus was hungry. His tears trickled down into his soup and no one had any power to comfort him. Still, neither Father nor Grandmother seemed particularly worried.

"She will come back, Dani," said Father quietly. "She's only hiding for today."

There was no sun either. Grey clouds hung low, hiding the mountains, and fresh soft snow began to fall.

At night it would harden into a crust and next day would be dangerous for walking. Father pulled on his cape and got out the big sleigh to haul in logs, Grandmother went to sleep in the armchair by the stove. Dani came and leaned against Annette and looked up into her face.

"Nette," he said, "I want to go to bed."

"Why, Dani?" asked Annette, astonished. "It's ever so early. It's only just beginning to get dark, and you haven't had your supper!"

"But I want to go to bed, Nette," persisted Dani. "You see, I want it to be time to say my prayers."

Annette gave a little laugh. "You don't have to go to bed to say your prayers, Dani! You could say them just as well now, and then have your supper and go to bed at the ordinary time."

But Dani shook his fair head.

"No," he said, "I want them to be my proper prayers in my nightshirt. Please put me to bed, Nette."

"Oh, all right," answered Annette, beginning to unbutton his jersey, "but you know, Dani, it doesn't really make any difference being in your nightshirt." Then she kissed him because his small face looked so terribly sad and his mouth dropped so at the corners.

When he was safely buttoned into his white starched nightshirt he knelt down and folded his hands and prayed for Klaus.

"Dear God," he prayed, "please bless Klaus. Please find her and bring her back to me quickly. Don't let her be cold, or hungry, or frightened. Show her the way home tonight. Please, please, dear God. Amen."

"Aren't you going to pray for anyone else?" protested Annette, in a slightly shocked voice.

"No," replied Dani, getting up from his knees in a hurry, "not tonight. I don't want God to think of anyone but Klaus tonight!" And then, thinking that he was being perhaps a little unkind, he added, "You can say the other people later."

Having committed Klaus into the hands of the heavenly Father, Dani climbed into bed with a peaceful heart, and pillowed his cheek on his hand. But he opened his eyes and said drowsily, "Nette..."

"Yes," answered Annette.

"You'll wake me when she comes, won't you?"

"When who comes?"

"Klaus, of course!"

"Yes, Dani. I promise."

"Thank you, Nette." And with that, Dani fell asleep.

Annette wandered round the room restlessly. Then, because her cheeks felt hot and because she had been indoors all day, she opened the door and went out onto the balcony.

It had stopped snowing. A west wind was coming up the valley, blowing the fresh soft snow across the old with a sound like a gentle sea. Already it was piling in drifts against the walls of the chalet. It was not a bitterly cold wind. It felt pleasant on her hot cheeks, and she decided to go for a walk up to the riverbed. She might meet Klaus.

She slipped on her cloak and set off. It was full moon and almost light enough to read by. As Annette reached the top of the field she turned and looked back over the snow and could see her footprints just like the footprints of the man in her dreams. Only his had stretched such a long way. He seemed to have travelled right across the world to reach that dark little house. And all for nothing.

17

Annette wandered quite a long way and at last she reached the little bridge that crossed the river. The railings were hung with icicles and the little river was almost silent. Only a whispering runnel deep below the white boulders told that the river still lived.

It was very still up there. The wind had dropped and it had begun to freeze – the little bridge was treacherously slippery. Annette, with her thoughts far away, never noticed the sheet of ice below the soft fall... until her foot slipped and she stumbled forward with a little cry of pain.

For a moment the pain in her ankle made her feel faint and sick, and she lay for a minute or two in the snow without moving. Then she tried to rise, but sank down again with another cry. She knew she had sprained her ankle badly, as she could not stand on it at all.

For a few minutes she felt terribly frightened. She was alone on the mountainside, and no one was likely to come down the lonely forest path that night. It was getting colder and colder. Unless she could reach shelter, she would certainly freeze to death.

Then she remembered that there was a chalet a little further up the mountain round the bend in the path, just inside the forest. A young woodman and his wife lived there. If she could drag herself on her hands and knees to their door they would take her home on their sledge. It was not very far. She would start at once.

She began crawling painfully through the snow, dragging her poor swollen foot behind her. It ached dreadfully at every jolt, and before long she began to get terribly tired. Her hands kept sinking into the snow, and her eyes filled with tears. Would she ever get there?

She had reached the hairpin bend in the path where the forest sprang up, and now, to her relief, she could see the chalet, not very far away, with one little light in the window. She felt she could go no further, and sank down in a drift to rest a little. But she soon began to feel cold and braced herself to struggle on.

Little by little she advanced, until after what seemed hours she reached the steps of the little house. She gave a low call, hoping that someone would come out. But no one came. So she struggled up the steps herself and sank down in an exhausted heap on the doorstep.

Then with a sigh of relief she stretched up and knocked on the door.

There was no answer. The little house seemed as silent as the snow and the windless woods. Annette reached up again and knocked as loud as she could.

But there was still no answer. Nothing stirred in the little house. No friendly footstep came towards her.

In a frenzy of fear, she staggered up on one foot. She beat on the door until her fists were sore, shouting at the top of her voice, and rattling the latch. Then, as the terrible truth dawned on her, she sank down on the steps and burst into frightened tears. The door was locked and the house was empty. The little light had only been left on to scare thieves. There was no one there at all.

For a few moments panic seized her, for she was a mountain child and had often heard of people being frozen to death in the snow. But then her panic left her and she began to think rapidly and reasonably.

If they had left the passage light on they probably meant to come back that night.

But if they had gone down to the valley they might be a long time coming, and then perhaps it would be too late. Already she could feel the cold creeping into the tips of her fingers. Perhaps if she rested a little she might be able to crawl back the way she had come. But the next chalet was a long, long way down, and the drifts were soft and deep.

Anyhow, she would wait a little and then try. It was her only chance.

She looked helplessly out into the wide untrodden waste in front of her. To her right lay the forest and the river. But to her left, the fields sloped down in an unbroken stretch to the valley, all the little walls and fences and hummocks buried and levelled by the snow.

Once again she thought of her dream. In her dream there had been footprints all the way to the door of the silent house.

And as she sat there waiting she thought of something else. She knew now, for the first time, what it felt like to knock at a closed door and get no answer.

She had knocked for only a few minutes. But the Lord Jesus went on knocking for years and years. She knew he did.

She had stopped knocking because she knew the house was empty. But just suppose Monsieur and Madame Berdoz had been sitting inside all the time. Just suppose they had heard her knocking out in the night and had looked at each other and said, "Somebody's knocking, but we won't let them in just now. We'll pretend not to hear. We won't take any notice!"

How angry she would have been with them. How much she would have hated them for being so unkind!

Yet that was exactly how she was treating the Lord Jesus. And he didn't hate her. He still loved her dearly, or he wouldn't still go on knocking and still want to come in.

She was thinking so hard about this that for a moment she almost forgot her fear and loneliness. But now she suddenly lifted her head and strained her ears, for surely she heard a sound.

It was a very gentle sound, but one that all mountain children knew well. The sound of skis running through soft snow! And then, the sound of a boy's voice singing.

Someone was coming down through the wood on skis. In a few seconds they would curve round the bend and shoot right past the front of the chalet. If they were going very fast they might not see her...

A little figure came into sight, swaying towards the valley as he took the curve, a thin veil of soft snow flinging up around him. Annette kneeled upright and shouted at the top of her voice.

"Help!" she cried, cupping her hand in front of her mouth. "Stop and help me!"

The skier, with a sudden outward twist of his body, turned and brought his skis to a standstill. Then he unstrapped them and ran lightly up the slope towards her.

"What's the matter?" he cried. "Who is it? Are you hurt?"

It was Lucien. He had been up the mountain to visit his old friend, and now he was on his way home. He had been startled by Annette's cry. When he saw who it was kneeling there in the moonlight he stood still and stared as though he had seen a ghost.

But Annette was too pleased to see anyone to care about who it was. Just for a moment she forgot everything except that she was found and saved. To her grateful eyes, Lucien might have been an angel straight from heaven. She stretched out her hands and seized hold of his cloak as though she were afraid he might run away.

"Oh, Lucien!" she cried, in a rather shaky voice. "I am so glad you've come. I've hurt my foot, and I can't walk and I thought I might freeze to death before Monsieur and Madame Berdoz came home. Can you take me home, Lucien? I'm getting so cold."

Lucien's big mountain cloak was round her in an instant. He squatted down beside her, and rubbed her cold hands.

"I can't take you on the skis, Annette," he said gently, "because you're too big to carry. But I can be home in five minutes now and then I'll come straight back with the big sledge and a rug. Then I'll have you at your chalet in less than half an hour."

And inside himself his heart was so full of sudden joy that he felt he must run and shout and sing. His dream had come true. He was doing something useful for Annette. She needed him. Now perhaps she would forgive him and forget that terrible quarrel.

"Won't you be cold without your cloak, Lucien?" asked Annette in a small, exhausted voice.

Lucien promptly took off his jacket and wrapped it round her head. He wished he might give her his shirt as well, although it wouldn't have been the slightest use. He could feel the bite of the frost on his body, and sped back over the snow, bracing his muscles and drawing in deep icy breaths. He had his skis on in a trice and skimmed the curve like an arrow released from a bow. The happiness in his heart was glowing so brightly that he was almost unaware of his numb body, until he stumbled into his home. How his mother cried out at the sight of his bare arms and blue nose!

Annette, left alone, snuggled up in the warmth of Lucien's rough cloak. He would be back in about 25 minutes and in those 25 minutes there was a good deal to make up her mind about.

Firstly, she was safe. Lucien had come out of the wood just at the right moment, and he had heard her cry. So all the time she had thought she was alone the Saviour outside the door had been caring for her and had sent Lucien to save her.

Secondly, she had discovered about closed doors. She was not quite sure yet just what would happen when she opened the door. But there was one thing she was quite certain about. She could not leave the Saviour outside any longer. She leaned her head against the snowy step-rail and closed her eyes.

"Lord Jesus," said Annette, "I'm opening the door now. I'm sorry it's been shut such a long time and you had to wait so long. Please come in now. I'm sorry I've hated Lucien. Please make me love him, and if I've got to tell about that little horse please make me brave enough. And thank you for sending Lucien to find me. Amen."

And so the Lord Jesus, who had been waiting outside the door of Annette's heart and life for such a long time, came in. He forgave all the things she had ever said or thought or done that were wrong, and gave her the power to live for him. There was no one there to see that wonderful thing happening. Even Annette didn't really feel any different. But up in heaven that night, Annette's name was written in God's Book of Life. And the angels were glad because another child on earth had opened the door and made room for the Saviour.

18

Well, thought Annette, I've done it, and now I know what's got to happen.

She found her heart beating very fast, and she looked up at the vast starry sky and the great mountains to steady herself. How big they were, how old and unchanging! They made her and her fears feel very small and unimportant. After all, they would soon be over and forgotten about, but the mountains and the stars would go on and on and on for ever.

A small dark figure appeared, running round the curve in the path dragging a sledge behind him. He had grabbed another coat, and was so out of breath with hurrying that he could hardly speak.

"Come on, Annette," he gasped. "I've brought the big sledge so there's plenty of room for you to stretch out your leg. We'll be home in a few minutes."

He held out his hand to help her get up, but she drew back. "Just a minute, Lucien," she said, in a hurried, rather shaky voice. "I want to tell you something before we go home. Lucien, it wasn't the cat that knocked over your horse that day. It was me. I did it on purpose because I didn't want you to get the prize, because you hurt Dani. And I'm sorry, Lucien."

Lucien stood and stared at her, too surprised and, strangely enough, too happy to speak. For instead of feeling angry he felt tremendously relieved. Annette had done something wrong as well! If he had to forgive Annette, perhaps it would be easier for Annette to forgive him. Of course a little smashed horse was nothing compared with a little boy's smashed leg, but even so, it seemed to bring them somehow nearer together.

But he couldn't put all that into words, so he just gave a gruff little laugh and said shyly, "Oh, it's all right, Annette. You needn't worry about it. I forgive you. Get on the sledge." Then he tucked the cloak round her, sat down in front of her, and together they sped down the mountainside. They arrived at the Burniers' front door powdered all over with the snow that flew up from the runners.

Annette climbed the steps on her hands and knees and stood on one leg in the doorway. Then she looked at Lucien, who was turning away slowly with the sledge.

She had opened the door of her heart to the love of the Lord Jesus, and that meant opening the door to Lucien as well. For she knew the Saviour's love never shut anyone out.

"Come up, Lucien," she called. "Come in and see Grandmother. She will be so pleased that you found me."

And she opened the front door as wide as it would go, and she and Lucien went in.

Grandmother jumped up with a cry of joy at the sight of Annette. She and Monsieur Burnier had been very anxious. Father had gone up the mountain to search for her. Grandmother was opening her mouth to be cross when she noticed Annette was limping. So she said nothing, helped Annette onto the sofa instead, and went to look for cold-water bandages.

But as she turned she noticed Lucien standing shyly on the threshold, and for a moment they stood looking at each other. Grandmother's dim old eyes could read the faces of children like open books. And in Lucien's she saw such repentance, such hungry appeal, such timid hope and dawning courage as she had never seen in any child's face before. She put both hands on his shoulders and drew him to the warmth and blaze of the open stove.

"You are welcome, my child," she said firmly. "Come and sit down and eat with us."

The door opened again, and Father entered, shaking the snow from his cloak. He had guessed Annette was safe for he had seen the sledge and the forms of two children whizzing across the fields. When he had heard her story and scolded her a little for going so far alone at night, he too sat down by the open stove. Grandmother served hot chocolate and crusty bread thickly spread with golden butter to them all. On top of each hunk she placed a thick slice of cheese full of holes, and everyone sat munching in silence.

A sleepy, contented silence! The warmth of the stove after the night air made them all feel drowsy. Lucien sat blinking at the flames and wished that this moment could last for ever. Then suddenly the silence was broken by an odd scratching noise on the door.

"It's Klaus!" shouted Annette, and sprang forward. But her sprained ankle held her back, and it was Grandmother, Father and Lucien who all opened the door at once.

Klaus marched into the room with her tail held proudly in the air. In her mouth was a blind, tabby kitten. Klaus took no notice of any of them. She walked straight across to the little bed where Dani lay sleeping and jumped up onto the feather quilt. She dropped her precious burden as near as possible to the tousled golden head, and then hurried back to the door and miaowed.

"She'll be coming back with another," said Father, letting her out.

"Then we had better leave the door open," said Grandmother. She hugged her shawl tightly round her shoulders and asked Lucien if he would kindly fetch the chamois skin and put it over her knees. Then they all sat shivering in an icy draught until Klaus reappeared in a great hurry. She dropped a smudged white kitten with tabby bracelets in the same place as the other and streaked off back into the night.

"Let us hope that this will be the last," murmured Grandmother, thinking partly of the draught and partly of life in a small chalet with Dani and lots of kittens. But nobody else said anything at all because their eyes were fixed on the door.

Back came Klaus round the corner of the barn, but this time she walked slowly and majestically. Her work was done. She carried in her mouth a pure white kitten, exactly like herself. She gathered all three between her front paws, laid herself across Dani's chest, and started licking the kittens and purring.

"Shut the door, Lucien," said Grandmother, with a little sigh of relief. "And Michel, you had better find a basket for all those cats. The child will suffocate!"

Father chuckled. "In the morning, Mother," he replied. "Tonight they can stop where they are. The animal knows where they're welcome, and Dani won't mind."

Very gently he moved Klaus' right paw from Dani's chin. Then he went off to lock up the cowshed.

Lucien got up to go. He went over to Grandmother and held out his hand.

"I must go," he said simply, "but thank you for letting me come in, and I hope Annette's ankle will soon be better."

Grandmother, looking into his face, held his hand for a moment in both hers. "Yes, you must go," she replied, "but remember, you are to come again. You will always be welcome."

Annette said nothing about waking Dani because Grandmother might have strongly disapproved. But she'd remembered that she had promised to wake him when Klaus came home. So she waited till Grandmother was washing up the chocolate cups and then she hopped to his side.

"Dani," she whispered, smoothing the damp hair back from his forehead. Dani sighed and flung his arms above his head but he did not wake.

"Dani!" said Annette, more loudly. He opened his eyes, bright with sleep, and stared at her.

"Look, Dani," said Annette, "she's come. And she's brought you some presents!"

Dani stared at the jumble of fur on his bed, too half-asleep to be astonished and not quite sure whether he was dreaming or not.

"She's found three rats," he exclaimed.

"No, no, Dani," cried Annette. "Those aren't rats! They're three little kittens. She had them in the barn and now she's brought them to you. They're yours, Dani. Presents from Klaus!"

Dani blinked at them. "I knew she'd come," he murmured. "I asked God."

Annette knelt by the bed and gathered the whole bundle of Dani and Klaus and the kittens into her arms.

"And I asked the Lord Jesus to come in," she whispered. "And he did. That's two prayers answered in one night!"

But Dani did not hear. He had fallen asleep again.

19

Grandmother's cold-water bandages were so successful that when Annette woke next morning the pain and swelling in her ankle were almost gone. But she found it still ached to walk. It had snowed in the night, too, and the drifts were so deep that Father had to dig a path to reach the cowshed, so it was not a day to go out.

But Annette and Dani and Klaus and three kittens together in the living room were just too much of a good thing. By the afternoon, Grandmother suggested they should all go over to the hay barn and play there. So Dani carried his new family across in a basket and made nests for them. Then he turned somersaults in the hay. Annette lay comfortably on her tummy and, with Grandmother's big Bible propped up in front of her, turned over the pages.

She wanted to find her own special verse about Jesus knocking at the door, which the pastor had read. She wanted to learn it by heart right through. She found it quite quickly because the pastor had told them that it came in the last book in the Bible. Here it was, in Revelation, chapter 3, verse 20:

"Listen! I stand at the door and knock; if anyone hears my voice and opens the door I will come in and eat with them and they will eat with me."

Annette learned it so that she could say it without looking, and wondered what the last bit meant about eating together. She must remember to ask Grandmother when she next got a proper chance. Then she rested her head on her arms and just lay thinking for a time and watching Dani. He looked very strange doing somersaults because his good leg curled up and his bad leg stuck straight out.

She had opened the door to the Lord Jesus and he had come in and was living in her heart by his Spirit. It had turned out as Grandmother had said. He had come in with his Spirit of forgiveness and love. The hard, angry thoughts had gone away like shadows before the light and it had suddenly not seemed difficult to forgive Lucien. In fact, she had stopped thinking very much about that bit of it, because when the Lord Jesus came in he had begun to show her how selfish and unloving and untruthful she had been herself. What she was really worrying about now was whether Lucien would forgive her.

She had told him, and he had not seemed cross. But, after all, he had lost his prize, and Annette knew now that there was still something more she could do about it, if she really wanted to.

There were the Noah's ark animals. If she took them to the master and told him all about it he would see how beautifully Lucien could make things. He would probably give Lucien another prize even now, if he really knew what had happened.

But she was so afraid of what the master would think and what the other children would say that she decided not to do any more about it. As soon as she decided that, she found she did not want to think about the Bible verse any more. It had stopped making her happy. She began swinging on the beams instead, feeding the cows through a hole in the board until Father came over to milk. Then she went down and sat in the manger and talked to him while he worked.

Darkness fell early, the children went in to their evening meal, and then it was Dani's bedtime. There was a commotion at bedtime because Grandmother wanted the kittens to sleep in the barn and Dani wanted them to sleep in the bed. In the end they each gave way a little, and the kittens slept under the bed. But there was a lot of conversation about it and by the time it was all over Grandmother felt tired out and sank into her chair with a little sigh. Annette drew her stool up beside her, but no sooner were they comfortably settled than there was a knock on the door, and Annette got up to open it.

Lucien stood in the doorway, twisting his hands together shyly. Annette, although she wanted to be nice, felt shy too, and they stood there awkwardly waiting for each other to say something.

Grandmother looked up, surprised at the silence.

"Come in, Lucien," she called. "We are glad to see you. Annette, draw up another stool and sit down, both of you."

They sat down obediently, and Lucien, after saying that he had come to see how Annette's ankle was, went quiet. Annette, after saying it was "Much better, thank you", sat staring at the floor. Grandmother looked at them both very hard over the top of her spectacles.

"Annette and Lucien," said Grandmother suddenly, "you must stop this quarrel, and behave like sensible children. Lucien, you did a terrible thing, but you did not altogether mean to do it, and you have suffered for it. It's no good crying over spilt milk. Now you must take courage and start again. Annette, you must learn to forgive and be kind and stop thinking yourself better than other people."

"I don't," said Annette.

"You do," replied Grandmother, "or you would not find it so difficult to forgive them."

"But I have forgiven him," replied Annette. "Out on the mountain last night. It wasn't very difficult to forgive, because I did something nasty to him as well. When I told him about it, he said he'd forgive me too, didn't you, Lucien? So we're as bad as each other."

"Yes," replied Lucien simply. "But it wasn't such an awful thing as I did. I can make another horse, but I can't make Dani a new leg. And, anyhow, everyone says you're good, and likes you. Nobody likes me."

"But perhaps," replied Annette, "it's because they all know what you did, and nobody knows what I did. And do you know, Lucien, this afternoon I was thinking I ought to tell the master, but somehow I don't think I should ever dare."

They were talking to each other. Grandmother sat listening, but because it was Grandmother they did not really mind. Now she spoke.

"Annette," she said suddenly, "how did you come to feel you could be forgiving? Two nights ago you told me you never could."

"Well, Grandma, I opened the door, like you said, and then it all happened just like you said. When I asked Jesus to come in it somehow didn't seem so difficult. Lucien, I used to hate you, and that's the truth. But when Jesus came into my heart… well, I started to like you."

"Yes," said Grandmother, "I knew it would be like that if you would only open the door. When Jesus, with his great love and forgiveness, comes into our hearts there just isn't room for unkindness and selfishness and unforgiving thoughts. They go, like darkness when the sun shines in. But there is something else besides unkindness that the love of Jesus casts out. Fetch my Bible, Annette."

Grandmother turned the pages slowly, peering at the print until she found the fourth chapter of 1 John. She pointed to verses 18 and 19.

"Read it, Annette," she said.

So Annette read aloud: "'There is no fear in love; perfect love drives out all fear. So then, love has not been made perfect in anyone who is afraid, because fear has to do with punishment.'".

"That's right," said Grandmother. "Perfect love sends away fear. When Jesus brings his perfect love into our hearts it drives out unkindness and selfishness, and it can also drive out fear. You see, if we really believe that Jesus loves us perfectly there is nothing left to be afraid of. If he loves us perfectly, he will never let anything really harm us."

Annette and Lucien sat thinking for a moment. Then they smiled at each other, and Annette got up and went to her own cupboard. She brought out her Christmas bear and broke it in half as a peace offering. They sat on their stools, Lucien munching happily, but Annette thoughtful and troubled. She knew more clearly than ever now what was right, but still she didn't want to do it.

Lucien didn't stay very long, and when he was gone Annette said goodnight and rose to go to bed.

"Annette," said Grandmother, "remember that when Jesus comes in, he only comes in as Lord. You must do what he tells you, and not what you want any longer."

"Yes, Grandma," said Annette rather sorrowfully. She went upstairs, and when she was undressed she knelt down to pray.

"Lord Jesus," she said. "I do want to do what you say. If I've really got to tell, please make me brave and stop me being afraid."

She got into bed with a lighter heart and soon fell asleep. In the morning she woke early, and lay in the shuttered darkness wondering what time it was.

As she wondered, sleepily, she saw a light creeping through a chink in the shutter and falling in a bright patch on the floor.

It's morning, thought Annette. I'll open the shutters and see if the sky is beautiful.

She jumped out of bed and flung them back and the light streamed in. The valley still lay in deep shadow, but the sunlight, rising over a gap in the mountains opposite, had crept down as far as their chalet. The light glistening on the snow was dazzling and the peaks behind so bright that it hurt to look at them. It filled the little room that had been so dark with the sweet, cold freshness of early morning.

Grandma spoke about shadows, thought Annette, and she was right. There's no way of getting the shadows out of the valley except by just waiting till the sun shines on them. Then you couldn't keep them if you tried. Hating Lucien is like shadows, and being afraid of owning up is like shadows. Letting Jesus in is like opening the shutters.

She was so pleased with this thought that she got back into bed and lay comfortably thinking about it until it was time to get up. Then, still limping a little, she dressed and went to the kitchen where Grandmother was stirring the coffee.

"Grandma," she said firmly, "I want to go and see the schoolmaster this morning."

"But what about your ankle?" asked Grandmother.

"I'll go on the sledge."

"But how will you get back?"

"I don't know. I suppose I'll just limp back. But whatever happens, Grandma, I must go and see the schoolmaster this very morning. It can't wait."

"What's all this about?" chimed in Father, who was knocking the snow off his boots in the doorway. "If

Annette wants to see the master she can come down with me. I'm taking the cheeses down to the train in the mule cart. I'll drop Annette at the house, and pick her up on the way back from the station."

Annette's face brightened. She just couldn't have waited. If she waited another whole day she knew she might start feeling terribly afraid again.

Sitting beside Father in the mule cart, with the cheeses bumping about behind her, and the Noah's ark animals wrapped carefully in her hanky, she didn't feel quite so happy. She couldn't imagine what she would say to the master! What if he was very, very angry with her? He might easily be.

"What do you want to go to see the master for?" asked Father suddenly. "Are you tired of having no lessons to do?"

Annette leaned her golden head against his coat.

"No," she replied shyly. "It's just something I want to tell him. It's a secret, Papa."

She slipped her hand into his, as it held the rein, and he, good, wise man that he was, smiled and asked no more questions. He was a very busy man, working hard from early morning till late at night to make his little farm pay enough to keep his children. He did not often have time to talk to them seriously. He left that to Grandmother. But he usually knew what they were thinking by watching their faces and listening to their ordinary chatter. And in the quiet of the cowshed and the forests as he worked for them, he thought about them and prayed for them. He knew that his little daughter had been miserable, that something had happened to her and that she had found peace. He was quite content to know that she was happy, without asking why and how.

They jogged on in silence, until the white house came in sight. In summer it looked spotless, but against the purity of the snow it looked dingy and grey.

"Down you get," said Father, "and I'll be back for you in about half an hour."

The mule lurched on, and Annette, with her heart beating very fast, walked up the path. She stood for a long time without daring to knock. In fact, she might have stood there until it was time to go home again if the housekeeper had not seen her out of the window and come and opened the door without her knocking.

"Annette!" cried the housekeeper, and then the schoolmaster appeared.

"Come in, come in," said the master genially. He took her into the little room where they had so often sat together as Annette completed the tests. He was a good teacher and in holiday time he missed his pupils and liked them to call on him. Annette went straight to the table and undid her handkerchief and arranged the little Noah's ark animals in a row.

"Lucien made them," she announced firmly. "Aren't they good!"

The master picked them up and examined them with interest. "They are beautifully done," he replied. "They are really exceptionally good for a boy of his age. He will soon be able to earn his living. I had no idea he could carve like that. I knew he entered for the handcraft competition but in the end, he seemed to change his mind. I wonder why?"

"It was my fault," answered Annette, still very firmly. "That's what I came to tell you about. He made a little horse. I smashed it when he wasn't looking because I was so angry about Dani. But I'm sorry now, and I wondered if he couldn't have a prize after all, now that you know all about it."

The master looked at her thoughtfully. Her cheeks were scarlet and her eyes fixed on the ground.

"But I haven't another prize," said the schoolmaster at last. "There were only two. One was given to Pierre and one to you."

"Then Lucien ought to have the one that was given to Pierre. It was for the best boy, and Lucien's was much better than Pierre's."

"Oh, no," replied the master, "we couldn't do that. After all, Pierre won quite fairly. We couldn't take his prize away. If you really want him to have a prize you will have to give him yours. It was your fault that he lost it, wasn't it?"

"Yes," said Annette. And she sat in silence for a full three minutes, thinking. Her prize was a beautiful book full of pictures of all the mountains in Switzerland. It lay in her drawer wrapped up in tissue paper and was her most precious possession.

Of course she could easily say no, and she knew the master would never force her to give it. But Grandmother had talked about perfect love. The Lord Jesus, with his perfect love, was living in her heart now, and he wouldn't want her to keep back anything.

"All right," said Annette at last.

"Good!" replied the schoolmaster, and there was a look of triumph in his eyes. Because in those three minutes he knew that Annette had won a very big battle. "You shall bring it to me when school begins. I will present it to him in class, and the children shall see his carvings."

"Very well," said Annette. She looked up timidly into his face to see if he thought her very, very bad. But he only smiled down at her, and she went away knowing quite well that the old master liked her just as much as he had before.

Back up the hill she went, with the empty mule cart bumping and jolting over the snow. Home again, and Annette climbed the steps and stood on the veranda. Dani came and stood beside her with his arms full of kittens. Behind her, Grandmother was cooking the dinner, and in front of her, the sun had reached the valley.

She gazed down at the glistening roofs and the silver river, felt Dani's warm little hand in hers, and smelt the delicious smell of steaming soup behind her.

This morning the valley was full of shadows, thought Annette to herself, and now it's full of sunshine.

And she knew it was like the Lord Jesus coming into her heart and filling her with love and light and courage.

20

Lucien climbed the hill with a light step, and Annette walked by his side. They had never walked home from school together before, but now it was different.

It had been a very happy morning for Lucien. The master, without explaining why, had suddenly said that he had seen such a good piece of woodcarving in the holidays that he had decided to award a further prize. To everyone's astonishment, Lucien had been called out to receive it. Annette, who had expected the master to tell the whole story, had almost fainted with relief. Then all the children had gathered round to admire the little wooden animals. Freckle-faced Pierre had admired them louder than anyone else, remarking merrily that it was lucky for him they were given in so late or he would never have won the prize. And everyone had heartily agreed. Then they had all wanted to see Lucien's book, and the girls had cried out, "Oh, it's just the same as Annette's book!" And Annette had waited uncomfortably for Lucien to say, "It is Annette's book."

But he only replied, "Is it really?" And when no one was looking, he had winked at Annette.

When they were well out of sight of all the other children, he held the book out to her.

"It was nice getting a prize after all," he said, "but I don't want to keep it. Truly I don't, Annette. It's your book, and I should hate to take it away from you."

Annette shook her head.

"No, you've got to keep it," she said. "The master said so. It's your book now."

"Well," said Lucien, "it really belongs to both of us, so I think we'd better share it. Supposing I have it this month and you have it next month and me the next after that?"

Annette brightened up. She wanted her book terribly.

"All right," she replied. "I'll do that if you like. On the first day of every month we'll change."

And so it became a custom that at five o'clock in the evening on the first of every month the possessor of the book would carry it solemnly to the neighbouring chalet and lay it on the table. This custom lasted all the year, and it was a good one. For each time they changed over they were reminded silently that real happiness came from forgiving and sharing and helping one another.

"Let's sit down on this woodpile and look at it," said Lucien. They brushed the snow away from the logs and sat down and turned over the pages, for Lucien had never seen it before. He was keen on mountains and often studied the guidebooks, and now he pointed out the different ways of ascent.

"That's the best way up the Matterhorn," he said eagerly, tracing out the path with his finger. "That's the way I shall climb it first."

They sat there a long time with the hot midday sun beating down on them, and the sky powder blue behind the white peaks. It was such fun looking at the pictures that they forgot about being late for dinner, until a little voice quite close to them said, "Annette, Grandma said I could come and meet you. Dinner's been ready a long time, and I've finished mine."

It was Dani, leaning heavily on his crutches, looking flushed and tired. Annette jumped guiltily off the woodpile.

"Dani!" she cried. "You mustn't come so far down the mountain. You'll never get back. We must go home at once."

They started slowly up the road, but Dani was very tired. He had never been so far alone on his crutches before. But he had kept thinking that he would see his sister round the very next corner, and had hobbled on. In the end Lucien picked him up and carried him, and Annette carried the crutches.

Lucien carried him right to the door of the chalet, but nobody spoke. A sort of shadow seemed to have come between Lucien and Annette. Both were thinking that however much they made up their quarrel, Dani still could not walk and nothing would give him back his good leg.

"My leg aches so," moaned Dani, as Annette carried him up the steps. "Put me on my bed, Nette."

So Annette laid him on the bed and gave him all his cats to play with. And she sat down and ate her bowl of cold potato soup. Father had gone back to his work, and Grandmother, after scolding her for being so late, went to the kitchen where Annette soon joined her. Grandmother was standing at the table skimming rich cream from bowls of milk, and Annette started to help her.

"What is the matter, Annette?" said Grandmother suddenly. "You look unhappy."

Annette didn't answer for a long time. Then she said, "Grandma…"

"Yes, my child?"

"Grandma, ever since I asked Jesus to come into my heart he has helped me to like Lucien, and taken away the unkind thoughts. And at first it was all right. But now when I see Dani with his leg hurting so, and remember he used to be so strong, all these thoughts come again."

"Yes," said Grandmother, "I expect they do. Every day of your life ugly, angry, selfish thoughts will knock at the door and try to get in again. Don't try and push them back yourself. Ask the Lord Jesus to meet them with his love. Think about the love of Jesus all you can. Read about the love of Jesus every day in the Bible. If you keep your heart full of it, there just won't be room for those thoughts to stay."

"Where in the Bible, especially?" asked Annette.

"All through the Bible," answered Grandmother. "We have been reading the Gospel of Mark aloud at night lately, haven't we? Every page is full of the love of Jesus – his love to his disciples, his love to his enemies, his love to all poor and suffering people, his love for little children. Read carefully to yourself all the story of the life of Jesus and think a great deal about the way that he loved. And remember that it's that same love that came into your heart when you asked the Lord Jesus to come in."

"Yes," answered Annette rather absently, and to herself she thought, I'll start today, and every morning when I wake up I'll read a story about how Jesus loved someone.

Lucien had gone home to his chalet, also thinking. The sight of Dani so tired made him sad. It was all very well for Annette; she had made up for the wrong things she had done, and had put it all right. But he could never make Dani's leg right.

Why had Annette forgiven him and been so different, he wondered, for about the hundredth time. At first he had thought it was just because he had found her in the snow, but now he knew it was more than that. She had talked about opening a door to Jesus, and her grandmother had said something about the love of Jesus turning out selfishness and unkindness.

The old man up the mountain had talked about mercy and forgiveness. Perhaps when you "opened the door", whatever that meant, mercy and forgiveness came in as well as love. Perhaps it was all the same thing.

Anyhow, opening the door had made a very great difference to Annette. She used to be so stuck-up and unforgiving. Now she was quite humble and kind. It made Lucien think that Jesus Christ was not just someone who lived long ago in the Bible stories, but someone who could really do things now.

He had been walking slowly, but he had nearly reached the chalet. Twenty minutes before, when he and Annette had sat down on the woodpile, the sky had been blue and still, but now large clouds were massing up behind the mountains, and a cold wind had begun to blow.

"It's blowing up for snow," said Lucien to himself. "There'll be a blizzard tonight."

The cattle were stamping restlessly in their stalls at the sound of the wind that had sprung up. Lucien went indoors quickly and joined his mother who was already eating her dinner.

"Come along," said his mother. "You're late. I'm glad you've no afternoon school because it's clouding over and I think we are in for a blizzard. What's that book you've got there?"

"It's a prize," replied Lucien. "The master gave it me for carving. He saw something I did in the holidays."

"Well, that was nice of him," said his mother. "Did he know about the other one being smashed?"

"Yes," answered Lucien and changed the subject. He did not want to answer awkward questions. He was going to keep Annette's secret for her.

His thoughts kept going back to her as he sat in the living room whittling away on a newspaper. His mother was ironing in the kitchen, so he was alone. "I asked Jesus to come in" – that was what Annette had said. Then her grandmother had asked Annette to read something out of the Bible… perhaps he could find it. He would like to read it again.

He went to the shelf and lifted down the dusty old family Bible with all the family births, marriages, and deaths written in the front. His mother did not often read it, and he did not know very much about it, except what he had learnt at school. He could not remember where the bit that Annette had read had come, but he thought it was somewhere towards the end.

He could not find it, but he found other things. He found the Gospels and the stories he had heard at school of Jesus the Healer – how he had made blind men see, and healed people with leprosy, and made dead men live. Yes, and there was a story about how he made someone walk!

"Get up! Pick up your mat and go home." Jesus had said that to a man who could not walk… and the man walked home!

Well, if Jesus was really alive today, and had changed Annette's heart, surely he could make Dani walk, too.

Lucien had never really said his prayers since he was a tiny boy and had sometimes said them to his mother. But now he slipped across to the cowshed, and ran up into the loft. He knelt down in the very same spot where, all those months before, he had wept so bitterly.

He did not understand yet what it meant to open the door to Jesus, but he believed now that God was near and would listen when he prayed. And now he prayed with all his heart that God would heal Dani and make him walk properly again, as he cured people in the Bible.

He stayed there quite a long time and then came down and milked the cows. When he opened the door to cross with the buckets he was nearly thrown back by the snow driven almost horizontally by the wind. His mother was at the window looking out rather anxiously into the dusk.

"There's a real blizzard," she said. "You'd better take the storm lantern and go to meet your sister. It's got dark so early."

But at that moment the door was flung open, and Marie, with the snow frozen on her hair and clinging to her coat, stood breathless and laughing in the doorway.

"It was a real fight with the wind getting up that slope," she panted, as she shook out her wet clothes and changed her boots. "I'm nearly worn out! Lucien, why didn't you come and meet me with the lantern? Mother, I hope supper's ready, because I'm famished."

They sat down at the table, Marie still chattering brightly with her cheeks as red as apples.

"What a day I've had!" she exclaimed. "People have been coming and going all day at the hotel. Not that they'll get much winter sport in this weather, poor things! I've been run off my feet. But I've had a good tip this evening. Look, Mother."

She pulled out a banknote and handed it to her mother. Madame Morel took it and smiled. She, like her neighbours, had difficulty in making the little farm pay, and Marie was a good girl about bringing home her wages.

"Who gave you all that?" she enquired.

"Oh, such a nice gentleman!" cried Marie. "And I believe he's very famous, too. The owner's wife was telling me about him at dinner. He's a very clever doctor and he can cure almost anyone with broken bones. He's got a hospital down by the lake, and people go there from all over Switzerland and he cures them."

Lucien nearly choked in his excitement. He leaned across the table.

"Marie!" he burst out. "Could he cure Dani Burnier?"

Marie stared at him in astonishment. She did not know that Lucien still troubled his head about little Dani Burnier.

"I don't know," she answered quite kindly. "They'd have to take him down to the lake if they wanted Monsieur Givet to see him. But they'd never have the money. Those clever men charge huge fees, Lucien. As much as all the Burnier cows put together, I should think."

Down to the lake! To Lucien, who had never left the valley, it seemed like the other end of the world.

He tried again.

"But, Marie, couldn't they take him to the hotel in the morning?"

"He's leaving on the early train. All his luggage was brought down tonight."

"But, Marie, couldn't they take him tonight?"

His earnestness touched Marie.

"Of course they couldn't, Lucien," she said quietly. "Fancy taking a little child out in this blizzard! Anyhow, the last train went hours ago, and the road over the Pass would be blocked on a night like this. It's quite impossible. Besides, I tell you they haven't the money! Stop worrying yourself about Dani Burnier, Lucien! You didn't mean to harm him really. And he's quite happy hopping about on those crutches, and getting thoroughly spoiled by that grandmother of his!"

Lucien said no more, and his sister went on to talk about the other visitors, and what the waitress had said to the porter, and what the owner had said to the cook.

Lucien didn't hear a word. He had quite made up his mind what he was going to do, but there were three mighty difficulties in the way:

1. The doctor's fees were very high, and Lucien had no money.
   His thoughts flew to the old man up the mountain. He had plenty of money if he could be persuaded to give it.
2. The Pass was probably blocked.
   Well, he could try. If he failed, he would know at least that he had done his best.
3. Would the doctor come? Would he not take the train that would carry him to his important hospital by the lake? Would he instead take a local train with a boy he didn't know, and climb the mountain in a blizzard to see a peasant child?

It was all most unlikely, but there was just a chance that it would work. Marie had called him a nice gentleman.

"I've finished my supper, Mother," said Lucien. "I'm going upstairs."

21

Once in his room, Lucien moved with great speed. There wasn't a minute to be lost.

He took his cloak from the cupboard and put on his woolly balaclava helmet that covered his ears. Then he wound his puttees round his legs and put on his stoutest boots. Then he wrote a note to his mother telling her he would not be back till morning.

He tiptoed down the stairs into the kitchen, and filled his pockets with bread and cheese and a box of matches. Then he silently lifted the latch of the back door and crept across to the barn. The storm lantern hung on the wall, and Lucien lit it and was comforted by its steady ray. He wondered whether to take his skis, but decided it was too dark. He opened the far door of the barn and stepped out into the windy snow meadows, and the blizzard nearly buffeted him over. He was safely away. His great adventure had begun.

If the wind was like this in the field, he wondered what it would be like on the Pass. Surely he would be blown over and buried in the drifts! Well, he would see when he got there. In the meanwhile he must think hard about reaching the old man.

It was a relief to reach the woods. Here, although the trees shuddered and tossed their branches and made eerie noises, he himself was sheltered. The snow on the path was less deep than the snow in the meadows. He could move more quickly without floundering.

Up and on he went through the tossing trees, until he could see a comforting orange glow of light in the old man's window. The end of the first stage of his journey was in sight. He braced himself to meet the wind as he came out in the open again, struggled to the old man's door and knocked.

"Who's there?" said the old man very cautiously from within.

"Me, Lucien."

The door was flung open instantly, and the old man drew him in.

"Lucien, my boy," he cried, peering at him in astonishment, "whatever brings you here, in this weather? What has happened?"

Lucien, after his battle with the wind, sank down on the bench for a moment to regain his breath. He did not like asking the old man for his money, but nothing must stand in the way of his quest.

"You once said," began Lucien, looking up into the old man's face, his eyes bright with anxiety, "that you had a lot of money to give to someone if they really needed it. I've found someone who really needs it. If you will give me your money I think little Dani Burnier's leg might be made better."

"How could that be?" asked the old man, looking very attentively at the boy.

"There's a doctor at the hotel where my sister works," explained Lucien, "who can cure people who can't walk, and heal broken bones. I'm going now to ask him to come and see Dani; but my sister says he would want a lot of money."

"You're going now?" repeated the old man, "in this weather? You must be mad, boy! You could never cross the Pass in this weather."

"I think I could!" replied Lucien doggedly. "The blizzard only started a while back, and the fresh snow won't be deep yet, if I hurry. But it's no good going unless I've got the money!"

The old man did not answer for a minute. He seemed to be struggling with himself.

"I would give it if I was sure of the man," he said doubtfully. "But I don't want to waste or lose it. How do I know that he is an honest man? What is his name, Lucien?"

"His name is Monsieur Givet. My sister says he's a famous man."

"Monsieur Givet!"

The old man repeated the words softly in a strange voice, as though he thought he must have made a mistake about them. It seemed to Lucien that he had turned rather pale. But without another word he turned away, took a key from one of his own carved boxes, and opened a little cupboard in the wall behind his bed. From this he drew out an old sock stuffed with notes.

"Take it all," he said, "and give it all to Monsieur Givet. Tell him it is all his if he will cure the child. Tell him… tell him, Lucien, that it is the payment of a debt."

His voice shook a little, and Lucien glanced at him in surprise, but he was too glad to wonder much. He had never seen so much money before in his life. He put the whole bundle inside his shirt, buttoned his coat and cloak over it, and made for the door.

"Thank you very, very much," he said hastily. "I'll come and tell you what happens."

The old man came to the door to watch him go, and held his lantern high to light the path. Lucien had gone only a few steps when the old man called to him loudly above the wind.

"Lucien!"

Lucien ran back.

"Yes, Monsieur?"

"You won't forget the message, will you?"

"No," replied Lucien carefully. "I'm to say it's the payment of a debt. I won't forget. Goodbye, Monsieur."

He was making off again into the night when the old man called again.

"Lucien!"

The boy ran back, impatient at the delay.

"Yes, Monsieur?"

"You won't tell him anything about me, will you? Don't tell him my name, will you, Lucien?"

"I don't know your name," Lucien reminded him.

"And don't you tell him where I live, Lucien! Promise me!"

"No, Monsieur, I won't tell him where you live," Lucien answered him, too impatient to wonder. "I promise. I'll just say it's the payment of a debt. Goodbye, Monsieur."

He sped off as fast as he could through the deep, soft snow, afraid that the old man might call him again. At the margin of the wood he turned and waved his lantern. Through the whirling snow he could still see the dim figure of the old man black against the light of his open door.

He must be very quick. The snow was still falling. Very soon the Pass would be uncrossable, if it were not so already.

He thought it probably would be uncrossable already on foot. He would go into the cowshed on the way down and get his skis.

He stumbled his way over the last field, sinking in at every step. The cowshed was mercifully still unlocked and Lucien stepped in with extreme caution. He had just lifted down his skis when the further door was flung open and his mother and Marie came in, waving a lantern.

Lucien propped his skis against the wall and fell flat on his face on the dirty floor behind the largest cow.

"He's not here," said his mother, flashing her lantern round the shed, her voice sharp with anxiety. "I believe you're right, Marie, he's got some mad notion about getting to that doctor. He'll be floundering along that mountain road by now, and the stupid boy hasn't even taken his skis. I wonder whether we could persuade Monsieur Burnier to go after him and fetch him back. He can't have got far on foot."

"I think we'd better," agreed Marie, and her voice sounded agitated, too. "Monsieur Burnier will easily catch him up on skis and stop him before he gets anywhere really dangerous. Let's go now and ask him."

They went off hastily, and Lucien, pressed against the cow's flanks, jumped to his feet. There wasn't a moment to lose.

It would take them two or three minutes to get on their mackintoshes and boots. In this weather it would take them a quarter of an hour to reach the Burniers' chalet and another five minutes while they told their story. Then Monsieur Burnier would have to collect his lantern and boots and skis. Lucien had roughly half an hour's start. It ought to be all right, but then he was only a light child and Monsieur Burnier a heavy, skilful man who could ski much faster than Lucien.

Very, very carefully, he crept from the shed, relit the lantern which he had blown out when he heard the latch move, and fastened his skis. Stemming carefully, he started off, holding the lantern out in front of him, his head well down because the blizzard was blinding.

Down over the meadows he went and then he reached the friendly shelter of the forest path where he could look in front of him. Out across the low fields skirting the village went Lucien, and here the wind was less furious and he could look straight ahead and go faster.

He made his way through the deserted village, looking anxiously round in case anyone should see him and want to know his business. But everyone was indoors on such a night. There was very little wind in the valley hollow where the village nestled, and poor buffeted Lucien enjoyed the lull. And the lights in the chalet windows gave him courage.

He crossed the silent market square with its frozen fountain and glided on downhill past the village dairy, past the station and over the bridge that led across the river. Then he paused for a few minutes to get his breath, for he had reached the very lowest part of the valley. Now he must start climbing the other side right up over the Pass that ran between two mountains.

He glanced back fearfully in case Monsieur Burnier should be following, but there was no one in sight. He suddenly felt terribly lonely, and longed for the village with its dark chalets and warm orange windows. For a moment he almost wished Monsieur Burnier would catch him up. But he pushed away the thought and began his climb.

The snow on the valley road was not too bad. Lucien shouldered his skis and found he could walk without very much difficulty. He could still hear the wind howling in the woods above him, but the blizzard seemed to be stopping.

He plunged into the woods and climbed, weary and afraid. These were not the familiar woods of his own side of the mountain, but dark, strange woods. Lucien was not even sure if he was still on the right path and, if he wasn't, it might simply lead him to the foot of a precipice. Somewhere, above the roaring wind, he could hear the angry rushing of a stream, and his skis seemed to get heavier and heavier.

He climbed through the woods for three hours, his mind full of fears and horrors. Every story he had ever heard about the perils of the mountains crowded into his mind – avalanches, treacherous drifts, breaking boughs. He thought of the St Bernard dogs trained to rescue lost travellers. Well, there were no dogs round here. He supposed he would just stay lost.

Unless of course, he chose to go back.

He stopped for a moment, wondering that the thought had not occurred to him before. How simple to buckle on his skis and stem carefully down the zigzagging forest path and go home!

"I did my best," he would tell them, "but I couldn't get through." And the Burniers would no doubt think it very heroic of him even to have tried.

The wind was roaring horribly and the great trees were crying aloud and tossing their arms. He was nearly at the top of the forest now, out on the wild wastes of the Pass where the wind might pick him up and whirl him over the rocks like a snowflake. He found his teeth were chattering and he was crying.

"I'm so frightened," he sobbed to himself. "I can't go on. I know I'll be killed on the Pass. I wish Monsieur Burnier would come."

And then as he stooped to buckle his skis he suddenly remembered that warm, sheltered moment, when he and Annette and her grandmother had sat round the stove together. Grandmother had talked about being afraid.

"Perfect love sends away fear … if we really believe that Jesus loves us perfectly there is nothing left to be afraid of. If he loves us perfectly, he will never let anything really harm us."

Lucien paused, with his hands on the buckles, stopped by his thoughts. So he was not alone after all. Annette's grandmother had said that Jesus loved him perfectly, and if he loved perfectly, he would not leave a child alone in darkness and danger. It was just as though someone stronger than the night, the wind, the terror, and the darkness had suddenly come to Lucien and taken his hand and pointed up the hill.

"Oh Jesus, please will you send my fear away?"

He shouldered his skis and went on.

"Perfect love sends away fear," he murmured to himself over and over again. It was true, too. He had stopped feeling so terribly frightened because he had stopped feeling alone.

He had reached the top of the forest and come out into the open, and now he could think of nothing at all except how to go on.

The wind struck him an icy blow, and he floundered straight into the new soft fall right up to his knees. He struggled out with difficulty, backed under the trees and buckled on his skis. Then, bent nearly double, because the pain of the cold wind on his face was more than he could bear, he struggled on.

Mercifully, it had stopped snowing and the sky was less inky. Now and again a pale moon broke through the ragged mass of hurrying clouds, and at such moments, if he lifted his face for an instant, Lucien could see rocks rising to his side, and knew that if he just went on straight in front of him he must reach the top of the Pass sometime.

And then, after what seemed a very long time, he was struck by a blast that sent him reeling backwards, and he lay gasping in the snow.

"I shall never be able to get up again," said Lucien to himself, almost too exhausted to care whether he ever got up again or not. And then once again he remembered about that perfect love, and because he felt the Saviour so close beside him, instead of praying, he just held out his hands to be lifted.

After a moment or two, a little strength seemed to come back to him and he struggled to his feet again. And he found that the ground in front of him sloped gently downwards. He had crossed the Pass.

Now he became thankful for the wind, because his legs were too weary and numb to steer his skis. Without that gale sweeping up the Pass against him, he would have gone dangerously fast. As it was, he travelled slowly, crouching for a little way, and then his legs crumpled up altogether and he sat down and let the skis carry him like a toboggan.

He was so cold that he had stopped feeling cold. Sitting there, sliding effortlessly down the hill, he wondered if he were going to sleep. A sort of drowsy numbness seemed to be stealing over him, until suddenly he felt a jerk and, coming to, he realised that the wind was no longer buffeting him and his skis had stuck in a drift.

He gave himself a shake and looked round. He had reached the forest again, and that was why the wind had dropped. He could not remember anything of the last few minutes. For all he knew it might have been the last few hours. But apparently the Lord in his perfect love had guided him, for the smooth forest track lay at his feet, winding away through the trees, and he had not missed his way.

He roused himself, for it was very dark and the storm lantern only gave light a little way ahead. He must steer himself carefully because the path zigzagged and he might fall over the edge or run into the tree trunks. But he was sheltered from the wind which had beaten the sense and feeling out of him. And that, for the moment, was all he cared about. He was beginning to feel that his limbs belonged to him again, and very painful they were!

Down, down, down. The forest was almost quiet now, for he was travelling towards a deep valley. Sometimes he stood, sometimes he sat. Towards early morning the clouds dispersed and the moon shone out, its light piercing the boughs. When at last he glided out into the open, the fields lay still and silver, and the dark town was below him. In half an hour's time he would be there, knocking on the door of the great hotel, and then... If Jesus really loves me perfectly, thought Lucien, he can't have let me come all this way for nothing. Too weary to think any more, he struck out across the meadows.

22

Monsieur Givet woke very early, and the first thing he thought of was that the storm had stopped, and the valley was still. The second thing he remembered was that he was going home today.

He was glad he was going home. He had been ill and had come up to the mountains for a week's rest and mountain air. Now he felt strong again and ready for work. Today he would travel on the early train and reach his lakeside home before midday. And what a welcome there would be! What a noise the children would make! He smiled as he thought of them: sturdy Marc; merry, curly Yvette; solemn Jean-Paul, and now baby Claire. And then he thought of their mother, merry and curly haired like Yvette but so often worn out by the end of the day. He wished he could find someone to help her. She had looked after the children alone since the nurse had left to be married a month ago. Well, when he got home he would see what could be done.

He got out of bed and dressed, and whistled while he shaved. Just as he was finishing there was a knock on the door.

"Come in," called Monsieur Givet, surprised, for it was much too soon for the early breakfast he had ordered. It was only about half-past five.

The door opened, and the night porter came in; he looked as though he had some rather mysterious news.

"Excuse me, sir," he began, holding his head enquiringly on one side, "but I suppose you weren't by any chance expecting a visitor?"

"A visitor?" echoed Monsieur Givet, still more surprised, "at this hour and in this weather? I certainly am not."

"Well, sir," said the porter warming up to his story, "it's like this. Just a quarter of an hour ago I heard a little rap on the door. When I opened it, there on the step stands a boy on skis, about 12 years old, sir, white as a sheet and looking more like a ghost than a boy. 'I want Monsieur Givet,' said he without so much as a good morning, and down he sits on the step and leans his head against the doorway. 'Well,' I says to him, 'you can't come calling on people at this hour of the morning, son! He's asleep in his bed.' 'I'll wait, then,' says he, and his head sinks down on to his knees.

"Well, I don't like to see a child taken like that so I took off his skis and dragged him in and sat him in a chair. 'Where have you come from?' I asked him. 'From Pré d'Oré,' says he. 'How's that?' says I. 'The early train isn't in yet.'

"'I came over the Pass,' says he. And, Monsieur, the more I look at that boy the more I feel like believing him. He's sitting down in the hall now. And when I passed your door, sir, and saw the light on I thought I'd come in and ask if you'd like to see him."

"I'll come and see him, certainly," answered Monsieur Givet, "but I can't quite swallow that story that he's just come over the Pass. I don't believe the guides themselves could have crossed last night. It must have been terrible up there."

The porter shrugged his shoulders, and led the way downstairs. But when they reached the hall they both ran forward together with a little cry of dismay.

Lucien had slithered off the chair and lay in a dead faint on the floor. His face looked very white.

Monsieur Givet picked the unconscious child up in his arms. "I'll take this boy to my room," he said to the alarmed porter. "You bring me some hot-water bottles and some brandy and some hot coffee. Be as quick as you can."

Upstairs in his room he laid the boy on his bed, removed his soaking boots and socks, and chafed his numb feet. Then the doctor took off the snow-crusted clothes and wrapped him in blankets. By this time, the night porter had arrived, puffing very hard, with the bottles and the brandy and the steaming coffee.

Monsieur Givet arranged the bottles and held a teaspoonful of brandy to Lucien's white lips. Lucien did not open his eyes, but he gave a tired sigh and swallowed the brandy.

"That's right, boy," said Monsieur Givet. "You'll soon be round."

When Lucien opened his eyes a few minutes later he looked straight up into a kind face, and couldn't think where he was. He felt deliciously warm and comfortable and drowsy. He thought he would never want to move again as long as he lived. But he would like to know who the man with the kind face was, who looked at him so intently.

"Who are you?" he murmured.

Monsieur Givet didn't answer at once. He raised Lucien's head and gave him some hot coffee. Lucien swallowed very slowly because it seemed too much of an effort to swallow just at the moment. When he had finished he said again, "Who are you, and where am I?"

"I'm Monsieur Givet," replied the doctor. "I don't know you, but I understand that you wanted me."

Lucien stared at him rather stupidly. He had been so tired that he had almost forgotten what he had come for.

But with the warmth and the coffee, things were beginning to get clear again, and at last he spoke.

"Are you a great, clever, famous doctor?"

"No. I'm just a doctor."

"But can you heal children who can't walk?"

"Sometimes I can. It depends why they can't walk."

"He fell over a precipice. He walks with crutches and a big boot."

"Who does?" asked the bewildered Monsieur Givet.

"Little Dani Burnier; he's 6. He lives in the chalet next to mine. So I came to ask if you could make him well. I've got enough money to pay you."

"But how did you hear of me?"

"My sister told me about you last night. My sister's a maid here."

"How did you get here in that storm?"

"I came over the Pass on my skis."

"You can't have done, boy, not in that blizzard."

"But I did. There's no other way to come."

It was quite true. There was not. Monsieur Givet sat looking at the boy as though he were some rare curiosity. As the doctor stared, Lucien's hand stole under the shirt he was still wearing and drew out the fat sock.

"Please, sir," he said, "would this be enough to make him better?"

Monsieur Givet drew out the contents of the old sock, and gave an exclamation of astonishment.

"Boy," said Monsieur Givet quite gently but very firmly, "before we go any further you must tell me where you got all this money from. Do you know how much there is?"

"No," said Lucien rather drowsily. "But my sister said you'd want a lot. Is it enough?"

"It's far too much," replied the doctor. "But where did you get it from?"

"An old man I'm friends with gave it to me," murmured Lucien, who felt he could not keep his eyes open another minute, "and there was a message. He said it was the payment of a debt, and you were to take it all."

"Who was this old man?" asked Monsieur Givet. "Just tell me that, and then you shall go to sleep. What was his name?"

"Please, sir, I don't know."

"Where does he live?"

"Please, he made me promise not to tell you." And with that, Lucien's eyes closed and his head rolled over on one side. He was fast asleep.

Monsieur Givet was in rather an awkward situation. His train was due to leave in three-quarters of an hour. But the boy lying on the bed had risked his life to come to him. It might be all for nothing, but he couldn't disappoint such determined courage by refusing to see the little child. And yet Lucien would probably sleep for hours now.

Monsieur Givet left the room softly, went downstairs to the telephone, and rang his wife.

"Are you there, Marthe?" he began. "Darling, I'm so sorry, but I shan't be home till late tonight. Such a strange thing has happened…" And, into her sympathetic ear, he poured the whole mysterious story.

As he left the office he was nearly knocked over by a girl – a red-eyed, pale-faced girl, in outdoor clothes.

"Oh, sir," she cried. "Porter tells me you've got my little brother safe upstairs. Oh, sir, Mother and I thought he was dead in the drifts. Oh, sir, I must go home quick and tell my mother Lucien's here."

Monsieur Givet sat down beside her on a sofa and tried to get some sort of an explanation out of her. But she could talk of little but the terrible night she and her mother had passed through.

Monsieur Burnier had been out all night looking for Lucien, but as they had told him that the boy had gone on foot, he had spent his time searching the edge of the woods. It would have been quite impossible for a child on foot to have come out into the deep snow meadows of the Pass, and the wind and blizzard had covered his solitary ski-tracks. Monsieur Burnier had come home with his sad news in the early hours of the morning.

Marie could tell Monsieur Givet very little about Dani. She was too upset to work, and now that she knew Lucien was safe she was in a hurry to take him home. She said she would telephone the post office and they would get a child to run up the mountain with the news so that her mother would hear more quickly.

But Monsieur Givet would not hear of Lucien going home just yet. Marie would go home by herself and when Lucien woke he would bring him on the train. Marie had better get someone to send a mule sleigh to the station as Lucien would probably be too stiff to walk.

Marie agreed to everything, and made off as fast as she could go, while Monsieur Givet went back to his room. Lucien still lay just as he had left him with his cheek resting on his hand. But there was a faint tinge of colour in his face. He looked much better. Monsieur Givet sat down and watched him, and wondered again how the boy had come into the possession of such an enormous sum of money. Who was the old man who had sent such a strange message?

"The payment of a debt!" Monsieur Givet decided to look into the matter very closely.

Lucien woke at midday, and once again could not remember where he was for quite a long time. He was aching in every joint, but it was a warm pleasant ache, provided no one wanted him to move. Monsieur Givet heard a little movement and came to see what was happening.

"Well?" he asked kindly. "How do you feel?"

"All right, thank you," answered Lucien. And then he remembered that he'd been to sleep, and added anxiously, "Will you have time to see the little boy I told you about, sir?"

"Yes," said Monsieur Givet sitting down beside him, "we'll go after dinner. I'll ring now for them to send up dinner for two. While we eat, you can tell me all about this little boy, and all about this old man who you say sent the money."

"I can't tell you about the old man, sir," replied Lucien, "because I promised not to. He's a sort of secret, and no one ever goes to see him except me. He said I was just to tell you that it was the payment of a debt and nothing else at all, sir. And he's been so kind to me, I couldn't break my promise."

"All right," said Monsieur Givet. "You shan't break your promise. I won't ask you anything more about him. Tell me about this little child. When did he hurt himself, and how did it happen?"

The doctor noticed that Lucien went very red. The boy didn't answer for a few minutes. He didn't want to tell his new friend what had really happened. But he realised that Monsieur Givet would be sure to find out from the Burniers, so it might be better if he heard it first from Lucien. So he replied, "It was my fault, really. It was last spring. I was teasing him. I pretended to drop his kitten over the ravine. Then, by mistake, I really did drop it. Dani tried to rescue it, fell into the ravine and hurt his leg and since then he's never walked properly, only with crutches. I thought perhaps..."

His lips trembled and his voice trailed off miserably into a whisper. But he had said enough. The doctor loved and understood children and in those few broken sentences he had grasped the whole story. He knew that this tired boy lying on the bed had been punished very bitterly.

"Lucien," he said, "we'll see this child together. It may be that God is going to make you the means of curing him. You know, Lucien, you have a great deal to thank God for. I think he must have been looking after you in a very special way last night or you would never have come across the Pass alive."

"Yes, I know," answered Lucien shyly and eagerly. "You see, only yesterday I prayed that God would make Dani better. And then when I heard about you, I thought it was the answer. But when I was in the forest I felt frightened and nearly went back. Then I remembered something I heard at Christmas and thought I'd go on instead."

"What did you remember?" asked Monsieur Givet, gently.

"I remembered something in the Bible," answered Lucien slowly. "It was something Dani's grandmother got his sister to read out. I can't remember it all, but it said that perfect love sends away all fear, and Grandmother said Jesus' love was perfect. So I wasn't afraid and I went on. I can't remember much about the top. But I got down safely."

"Yes," replied Monsieur Givet; "I don't think anything but the perfect love of the Lord Jesus could have sheltered you in that storm, or guided you on the right road, or kept you from being too afraid to go on. He's been very, very good to you, Lucien. Let's thank him now, before our dinner comes."

So Lucien buried his face in the pillow and Monsieur Givet knelt by the bed and prayed. He thanked the Saviour for his perfect love, stronger than storm or tempest, which had guided Lucien's steps through the darkness and saved him from fear and death. Then he prayed for little Dani, that God would give him, the doctor, skill to heal that leg.

Lucien, with his face still in the pillow, prayed as well, only not aloud. "Lord Jesus," he cried in his heart. "You were so near me on that mountain and I wasn't afraid. Don't go away again. I want to open my door like Annette did. Please come in."

23

Monsieur Burnier met the train himself, with his own mule sleigh, and drove Monsieur Givet and Lucien up to the chalet. All the villagers came to their front doors to see the doctor pass, as everyone had heard the story. Monsieur Givet had grown in fame and magnificence every time it was repeated. The children almost expected him to carry a magic wand, at a touch of which little Dani Burnier would be immediately healed. Lucien was spoken of as though he were some modern miracle. But he could not hear what everyone was saying because the mule was trotting fast and the bells were jangling loudly. That was a very good thing, thought his mother, afterwards, for listening to such things would have made him vain.

He sat on the sleigh, propped up against Monsieur Givet. He could not have walked a step if he had tried. He had had to be lifted from the train. His limbs were so stiff that they refused to function at all. But in spite of his weariness, he felt well and happy and full of hope. His heart seemed to be chiming as merrily as the mule-bells as they neared the chalet.

Monsieur Burnier sat silent in the driver's seat, not knowing what to make of it all. It was rather a responsibility having such a famous man on that sleigh. He only hoped that the mule, who was very frisky that day, wouldn't tip the sleigh over the edge on one of the corners. This was an event which happened fairly frequently, for the sleigh was very big and the path very narrow.

He was worried about the money, too. Of course, he would give all the money he possessed to see Dani cured. But he didn't possess very much money and what if it wasn't enough? Perhaps this very famous man would accept a young bull by way of payment.

Fortunately they reached the chalet without any adventures or upsets, and Monsieur Burnier helped the doctor to get down. Then he lifted poor Lucien in his strong arms and carried him up the steps into the living room, where he laid him on the couch. He, too, was pleased to see Lucien, for he had spent a weary, anxious night searching for him in the drifts.

Grandmother, Annette, and Dani looked rather formal and awkward. They were all dressed in their very best, sitting in a stiff little group on the edge of the best chairs. They looked as though they had been sitting there expecting the very famous man for a long time. When he entered, Annette and Dani looked at Grandmother and rose gravely to their feet. Grandmother, on account of her rheumatics, merely bowed her head.

Dani was not at all pleased. He had thought that a very famous man would be dressed in a scarlet robe like the overlord who made William Tell shoot the apple, in Annette's Swiss history book. He'd thought he would have a splendid curling yellow beard, too, and probably ride a white warhorse. But this stranger who came in behind Father was too ordinary for words. Dani felt very cross and stuck out his bottom lip and scowled.

The doctor sat down on a chair as far away as possible from the group and smiled at them. He had a nice broad smile, and Dani forgot his disappointment and smiled back.

Monsieur Givet put his hand in his pocket, withdrew a caramel and held it out.

"Do you want a caramel, Dani?" he asked.

Dani grinned happily and nodded his yellow head. He thought a caramel was much better than a scarlet robe and a warhorse.

"Come and fetch it, then," said Monsieur Givet, and Dani hopped delightedly across the room. While he hopped, the doctor watched him with the closest attention. When the child reached him he put the caramel into his mouth.

He liked this family immensely. He liked Grandmother, who leaned forward and watched him so shrewdly. It was as if she was saying, "That child is mine. Be careful what you do to him, or you will have me to reckon with!" He liked Father, with his honest, tanned face and his shoulders bowed with labour. He liked Annette, with her corn-coloured plaits and her spotless striped pinafore. Most of all, he liked the chuckling, friendly, blue-eyed little person who sat noisily sucking a caramel before him. He noticed too that there was no mother, and wondered whether it was the old woman or the little girl who kept the chalet in such perfect order.

"Does your leg hurt you?" asked Monsieur Givet.

"No," answered Dani.

"No, Monsieur," corrected Grandmother.

"Monsieur," added Dani, who was always obliging. "Only sometimes, when I walk without my crutches. My crutches have got bears' heads on them. Would you like to see them?"

"Very much indeed," said Monsieur Givet, and as Dani hopped over to fetch them he again watched him carefully.

"I can do enormous great hops on my crutches," announced Dani, who was not modest. "Would you like to see me do an enormous great hop?"

"Yes, please, I should," answered the doctor.

"Be careful of the chairs, Dani," chimed in Grandmother, who had forbidden Dani to do enormous great hops in the house. Annette hastily cleared Klaus out of the way, for there was no knowing where Dani might land.

The hop was a huge success, and the doctor clapped his hands. "Well done," he cried. "That was exactly like a kangaroo I once saw at the zoo. Now put down your crutches and walk to me without them."

Dani limped towards him, smiling, but dragging his bad leg rather pitifully. Monsieur Givet smiled back and gave him another caramel.

Only then did Grandmother, who had been watching very closely, turn to Annette.

"Annette," she said, "put the kettle on and make a pot of tea and bring the biscuit tin." Grandmother did not believe in pandering to the great until she was sure they really deserved it.

While Annette was getting tea, Monsieur Givet laid Dani flat on the table, and twisted and turned his leg about for a very long time. In fact, when he had finished, the tea was ready and Grandmother invited him to sit down and drink with them. He sat down and seemed lost in thought.

"Well," said Grandmother at last, rather sharply. "Can you do anything for him?"

Every eye in the room was fixed on the doctor as they waited for his answer. The only one who didn't look at him was Dani, whose eyes were fixed on the bricelet biscuits. They had forgotten to pass him one and Grandmother would be cross if he got up and helped himself. Bricelet biscuits were delicious, thin and crisp and golden, and Grandmother made them once a month in a special grill.

Monsieur Givet did not answer at once. He turned to Dani instead.

"Dani," he said, "would you like to be able to run about like other little boys?"

Dani hesitated. He was not quite sure. He was the only boy in the village who possessed bear crutches, and it made him a very special person. Then he remembered that spring was coming. Unless he could run about he would not be able to chase the baby goats in the meadows as he had done last year. And chasing baby goats was such fun that perhaps it was worthwhile being ordinary.

So he said, "Yes, thank you, I would. And please, Grandma, may I have a bricelet biscuit?"

But no one answered. Lucien and Annette were sitting with their cups poised in mid-air and both were rather pale. Everyone was still staring at Monsieur Givet.

"Dani," said the doctor suddenly, "where's that fine cat gone?"

"To the woodshed," said Dani. "Would you like to see her? She's got three kittens, too."

"Yes, please," answered Monsieur Givet. Dani limped off to find Klaus. And as he passed the table, he helped himself to two bricelet biscuits, and nobody even seemed to notice.

As soon as the door had closed on Dani, Monsieur Givet turned to Father.

"I think I may be able to help you," he said, leaning forward and speaking very earnestly, "although I can't tell for certain until I've seen an X-ray of it. I think the bone was never properly set and has joined up wrongly, and that I could break it again and pull it out straight. But it would mean an operation and a long stay in hospital. Would you be willing to let him come?"

Father rubbed his hands together miserably. He looked helplessly at Grandmother, and then at Annette. Operations had never come Father's way before and the word sounded horrible. Besides he had been told that operations were very expensive, and he wouldn't be able to pay.

"How much would it cost?" he asked at last, scratching his head.

"It wouldn't cost you anything," replied Monsieur Givet. "Lucien has paid for it himself, in any case. I can't explain now because your little boy will be back and we must decide before he comes. Will you let me take him?"

"Yes," replied Grandmother, who hadn't been asked.

"When?" asked Annette.

"Tomorrow morning," replied Monsieur Givet. "I shall be catching the early train, and I'll take Dani with me."

"Where am I going in the train?" said a clear voice. Dani had come in quietly through the back door and no one had noticed him. Now he stood at Monsieur Givet's elbow with his arms full of kittens, looking pleased. He had only once been in a train in his life, just for ten minutes, but he had never forgotten it.

No one answered. They were still staring at Monsieur Givet.

"Where, Grandma?" asked Dani again.

The doctor turned to Dani.

"Dani," he said, "you're coming with me down to the lake. You're going to stay with me for a little and I hope I'm going to make your leg better. Will you like that?"

Dani looked suspicious.

"And Annette?" he said firmly. "And Grandmother and Papa and Klaus and the kittens? Yes, Monsieur, we shall all like it very much."

"Oh, no, Dani," cried Annette. "We can't all come too! You've got to be good and go by yourself. Monsieur will look after you and you'll soon come back." But she was nearly crying as she spoke.

The effect of these words was terrible. Dani flung himself, kittens and all, into Annette's arms and burst into the most deafening roars of rage and despair.

Never had the Burniers heard such a noise. Annette hugged and kissed his top half, Grandmother shook and jostled his lower half, Father pressed handfuls of bricelet biscuits into his clenched fists, but nothing helped. The family looked at each other helplessly. Monsieur Givet knew that unless he could think of something very quickly, Dani would not be going with him.

He turned to Grandmother.

"Does the little girl know anything about looking after children?" he shouted above the din.

"She brought this child up!" shouted back Grandmother. This did not seem to Monsieur Givet a very good testimonial just at that moment.

"You had better send her with her little brother then," yelled Monsieur Givet. "She can help my wife."

"Dani!" screamed Annette, shaking him hard to make him listen. "I'm coming, too!"

Dani stopped his crying instantly, gave three hiccups and smiled. Monsieur Givet did not smile back. He looked at the little boy and spoke to him gravely.

"I'm afraid you are very spoilt, Dani," he said. "When you come to my hospital you will have to do what you are told without any fuss or screaming."

"And Annette!" Dani replied, and smiled again. He knew he had come out on top this time.

Monsieur Givet spoke to Monsieur Burner. "I am going to take Lucien home, if you can lend me a sledge," he said.

"So I will say goodbye for the present. The two children will meet me on the platform at 8.30 tomorrow morning with all that they need for the next two or so months. Annette shall help my wife in the morning, and attend evening classes for her schooling. In the afternoons she can be free to be with her little brother."

Father shook hands dumbly and wiped his brow. Events were moving so fast that he felt he had been left behind. But he was just beginning to understand that for two months, starting tomorrow, he had got to live without Annette and Dani, in a silent, tidy chalet. The desolation of that thought blotted out everything else. He went stumbling over to the cowshed to milk and to try to think things out, with his bewildered head pressed against Paquerette's warm flanks.

Grandmother said goodbye at the door, and held the doctor's hand for some moments in her own. "You are a good man," she said suddenly. "God will reward you."

Monsieur Givet looked at the valiant old woman in front of him, and his eyes suddenly became misty. He saw her with her two happy healthy grandchildren behind her, and the clean peaceful home of which she was the guardian angel. He caught a glimpse of the love and courage that had strengthened her gnarled hands, and lightened her dim eyes to perform a labour far beyond her natural power. And he saw the simple selflessness that gave up the children without question because it was best for them to go. He knew that he was standing face to face with one of the saints of God.

"You, too," he replied, "are a good, unselfish woman, and will most certainly find your reward."

Monsieur Givet pulled Lucien to his own chalet on a borrowed sledge, and carried him in to his mother. She pretended to be very angry with him.

"You naughty boy, Lucien," she cried, "going off like that and giving us all such a dreadful fright! How could you do such a thing?" But she took him almost roughly from Monsieur Givet's arms, helped him up the stairs, and put him to bed herself. Then she came back, sat down at the table, flung her black apron over her face and began to cry.

"You have a very brave son, Madame," said Monsieur Givet.

"He's a very naughty boy," snapped Madame. And because she was so terribly proud of Lucien and so glad to see him safe, she began to cry even harder.

She and Marie had been baking a big batch of Lucien's favourite cakes all the morning, and the house was full of the good smell. They invited Monsieur Givet to sit down and eat with them. But he refused because he still had something important to do and time was getting on.

"I believe," he began, rather abruptly, "that Lucien knows some old man round here. Can you tell me where he lives?"

"An old man?" repeated Marie. "Oh, yes, that would be that old man up the mountain who teaches Lucien woodcarving. They spend hours together, although what they talk about, goodness knows!"

"Can you tell me the way to his house?" asked Monsieur Givet.

"Yes," replied Marie, surprised. "It's straight up through the forest. But I shouldn't go up there if I were you, sir. The path will be bad after all this snow."

"I have business with him," replied Monsieur Givet briefly. "Perhaps you will point out the path to me from the door. On the way back down I will come and say goodbye to Lucien."

Monsieur Givet thought he had never seen a forest more beautiful as he toiled up the track that late afternoon. The trees were bowed down and the cones frosted and starred. What must it be like, thought Monsieur Givet, to be this old man and live alone among all this silence and peace, sharing the secrets of the forests, and watching the coming and going of the unhurried seasons? He began to look forward to meeting him, and found his heart was beating faster than usual.

As he left the forest he could see the small chalet with the snow piled high against its walls. The old man had dug a little path as far as the trees, almost as though he were expecting a visitor, thought Monsieur Givet, picking his way along it.

He knocked softly on the door and opened it without waiting for a reply. The old man sat hunched up over his stove whittling wood and drawing at his pipe. The goat and the cat sat either side of him for company, and Monsieur Givet took the chair the other side of the stove.

"Well," said the old man, still not looking up, "did you get there safely, Lucien?"

"It's not Lucien," replied Monsieur Givet softly. The old man jumped and looked up. And then they sat staring at each other as though they had each seen a ghost. And yet uncertainly, as though the ghost might possibly be real after all.

"I have come to give you back this money," said Monsieur Givet at last. "I don't want money to help that child. In the circumstances I will do it free, if it can be done."

"Then the boy broke his promise," growled the old man, and he leaned his chin on his stick and stared and stared and stared.

"He did not break his promise," replied Monsieur Givet. "He told me nothing but that it was given him by an old man, and that it was the payment of a debt. But I do not accept large sums of money from peasant boys without making sure that they were come by honestly. I had no difficulty in finding from other people where you lived."

There was another long, long silence. Then the old man spoke. "Is that all you came to say?" His voice sounded suddenly old and weary and hopeless.

Monsieur Givet got up quickly and knelt down beside the bowed figure of the old man.

"Now I see you, I know who you are. Need we pretend any more?" he said. "Let me take you home, Father. How much we've missed you and wanted you!"

24

A few hours later Annette, muffled in a woolly hood and cloak, sat in a big wooden rocking chair, smiling at Lucien. He was sitting up in bed with his chin resting on his knees. He was still rather pale and tired, but otherwise well and happy.

"Tell me all about it," urged Annette, her eyes big with admiration and astonishment. "Everyone says it was terribly brave of you. Tell me right from the beginning, Lucien, and what it was like on the top of the Pass."

Lucien wrinkled his forehead. It was nice to be called brave, and he would have liked to make a good story of it. But somehow it all seemed very far away and difficult to talk about, almost as though it had been a dream. He did not realise that his body had been too cold and weary to let his mind notice anything much.

"Well," he began, "I went up to the old man first and asked him for some money, and then I got my skis on the way down and skied down to the valley, and climbed through the woods across the river. And then when I got to the top it was very windy, and then I went down the other side."

"Of course you did," interrupted Annette impatiently, "or you'd never have got there. But tell me about it properly, Lucien. What did you feel like? Did you have any adventures? Were you frightened, and did you nearly die? And what was it like on the top of the Pass?"

Lucien was silent for a few moments. All the afternoon he had been wondering whether there would be a chance to tell Annette. But now the chance was here he didn't know how to begin.

"I was frightened," he said at last, rather slowly, twisting his fingers in the sheet. "Very, very frightened a little way before the top. I nearly came back. Annette, do you remember telling me how you used to hate me so and how you asked Jesus to come into your heart and how he made you like me instead?"

"Yes," replied Annette eagerly, "of course I remember. Why, Lucien?"

"Because," went on Lucien shyly, "something like that happened to me when I was feeling so frightened. I remembered what your grandmother said about perfect love sending away fear, and I asked Jesus to send mine away. I stopped feeling so scared almost at once."

"Did you really?" said Annette, deeply interested. "Then I suppose Jesus came into your heart as well as mine. And then your being afraid had to go away just like my hating had to go away. I suppose it's all really the same, Lucien, whether you're afraid or don't like people, or whether you cheat or don't speak the truth... whatever's the matter with you, when Jesus comes in I suppose there just isn't room for it any more."

"Yes," agreed Lucien thoughtfully, "I suppose you could say perfect love sends away fear or being selfish or telling lies or being lazy or cross or anything else that's horrible. When Jesus comes in, perfect love comes in too, doesn't it?"

"Yes," said Annette, "I suppose it does." And they sat with their chins resting on their hands and talked about it in the strange white dusk of twilight on snow. And neither suggested turning on the light, because it was nicer talking in the dark.

It was not till Annette was walking home across the starlit snow, with the great arms of the mountain thrown about her, that she fully realised that this was her last evening at home for a long time. And as the realisation came, she found she had a sudden pain in her throat and her eyes were misty. She broke into a fast run and arrived panting into the warmth of the living room.

Father was still over in the cowshed, but Grandmother was sitting sewing a button on Annette's clean striped pinafore. Annette and Dani's clothes, neatly folded and mended, were tied in two bundles on the table all ready for morning. Dani lay fast asleep in the bed in the corner with all his kittens on top of him as a last treat.

"Grandma!" cried Annette. She ran straight into the old woman's arms and burst into tears.

Grandmother let her cry for a little. Then she drew up the stool, and Annette sat down and leaned against Grandmother's knees while Grandmother talked. She talked about the home Annette was going to, the work she would have to do, and the joy of seeing Dani made well. She talked so cheerfully and bravely that Annette felt cheerful and brave too. She never knew that deep down in her heart Grandmother was saying to herself, "What shall I do tomorrow night and all the nights after when the stool at my feet is empty, and there's no little sleeping boy in the bed in the corner?"

And then, because it was getting late and they must be up early, Annette fetched the big Bible from the shelf as she always did at bedtime.

"We'll read the thirteenth chapter of 1 Corinthians tonight," said Grandmother, as Annette rested the great book on her knees. "It is a chapter I should like you to remember all the time you're away."

So Annette read it right through, and when she had finished Grandmother said, "The verse I want you to take away with you and remember specially is verse four. Read it again, Annette."

So Annette read it again, slowly and carefully.

"Love is kind and patient, never jealous, boastful, proud...".

"Now," said Grandmother, folding her hands on the Bible and looking at Annette through her spectacles, "you tell me that you have asked the Saviour into your heart, and he has come in and brought his love with him – the kind of love we were reading about.

"You're going to look after little children, and you're only a child yourself. They won't always be good with you. Often you will feel cross and impatient and bad - tempered. But the love of Jesus is kind and patient. Ask him to meet those cross bad-tempered thoughts with his love and you'll find they won't stay long.

"You are going to a big house, and you will see fine things that you will never own. Sometimes you may feel discontented and jealous. But remember, the love of Jesus in your heart is never jealous. If your heart is full of his love, there won't be room for discontent.

"You are going to be a little servant in a house of children. I don't suppose you will always get much notice taken of you. Often you will want your work to be seen and praised and made a fuss of. But remember the love of Jesus in you never pushes itself forward and never wants to be noticed, for it is not boastful or proud. His love can make you go on doing your work quietly and faithfully whether anyone notices you or not. Remember, he is your Master, and you are working to please him.

"Keep your heart full of the love of Jesus. Read about it and think about it. And when wrong thoughts knock at the door, don't try to keep them out yourself. Ask the Saviour to open the door for you, and tell them there is no room for them in a heart that is full of his love. Then they will have to go away!"

"Like the dark when you let the light in," agreed Annette, thoughtfully fingering her plaits. Then she kissed her grandmother and ran across to the cowshed to spend with her father the last half hour before bed.

Early next morning, at the hour when the valley was grey and the peaks silver, the whole family drove to the station in the mule cart. They arrived half an hour too early because they were so afraid of missing the train. So they stood on the platform among the milk churns, watching the light creep down towards the forests and waiting for Monsieur Givet. He joined them some twenty minutes later. Annette carried their luggage in a big brown paper parcel. Her hand was clasped tightly in her father's.

Dani, in his cloak and hood, seemed strangely shy, and kept edging off behind the milk churns. He looked anxious and seemed unwilling to be hugged when it came to saying goodbye. But the train was already far down the valley before Annette understood why. Then she noticed strange movements under the cloak as though Dani was having severe hiccups.

"What is that under your cloak, Dani?" she asked, gazing in astonishment at the heaving garment.

Dani went red.

"It's only one, Nette," he replied nervously.

"One what?" asked Annette, glancing anxiously up at Monsieur Givet. But the doctor, deep in a book, was not attending.

"Just him," explained Dani and undid a button. The face and whiskers of a white kitten appeared in the gap for an instant and then withdrew into its warm shelter.

"Dani!" cried Annette, "you're a very, very naughty boy! You know Grandma said you couldn't have kittens in hospital. I don't know what we shall do with him."

Dani gazed thoughtfully out of the window and said nothing. He couldn't think of a single excuse for what he had done. But under his cloak he gave the white kitten a secret squeeze. The white kitten curled his warm body against Dani's and purred, and neither of them felt the least bit sorry for Dani's crime.

25

Dani went straight to hospital when they reached the town. He was taken to a large room full of children like himself, who couldn't walk properly. There was a rather weary-looking nurse in charge. Dani took one look at the other children and decided they needed cheering up. So he offered to do kangaroo hops on his bear crutches all down the ward. It was a great success and within an hour Dani was friends with everybody. The white kitten was given a basket in the kitchen, and was to be allowed in during visiting hours.

Annette's arrival was not quite so happy. She was welcomed kindly by Madame Givet, who was young and pretty and merry, and taken to her room at the top of the house. When she was left alone, she ran across the room and looked out of the window and saw houses and slushy snow in the streets and low grey skies. She gazed for a moment and then flung herself on the bed and wept bitterly for the white stretches and clean peaks and clear skies of home.

Here Madame Givet found her half an hour later, when she came up to see what had happened to her. She said nothing, but slipped away and returned with baby Claire in her arms, and laid her down on the bed beside Annette. She could not have done anything better. Five minutes later, Annette was sitting up smiling with baby Claire chuckling and wriggling on her lap. And in yet another minute, Annette was chuckling back.

She was happy and busy at Monsieur Givet's house. In the morning she helped Madame and looked after the children, in the afternoon she sat with Dani, and in the evenings she did her lessons. The children were not always good with her, and often, to begin with, Madame Givet would have to be sent for to keep the peace. But although Annette sometimes felt cross and impatient with them, she tried hard to remember what she had learned from Grandmother's Bible reading.

"Love is kind and patient," she would say to herself desperately when Marc refused to do up his boots, Yvette spilt ink all over the floor, and Jean-Paul ran away and fell over in the mud. Gradually the love of Jesus in her began to make her patient and kind and unselfish, and she found that she could speak gently and keep her temper.

Dani was in hospital a week before he had his operation. He went off to the operating room in an interested and rather excited frame of mind, and went fearlessly to sleep. But when he woke up hours later he was very upset to find that his bed had been tipped up and there were large iron weights on the end of his leg, which hurt badly. He felt sick and hot, and screamed for Annette. When the nurse came he yelled at her for not being Annette.

All that week Dani lay on his back, with the weights hanging on his leg, feeling feverish and miserable. Annette came every day and read to him and told him stories about the white-sailed ships on the lake outside the great glass doors. She tried to make him forget how badly his leg was hurting him. But it was a miserable week. Dull clouds hung low over the grey waters of the lake, and Dani tossed and fretted and tried to be brave, but couldn't manage it.

But in those long days there was just one thing that comforted him. On the wall opposite him was a picture, with some writing under it that Dani couldn't read. When he was tired of the pain, and tired of stories, and tired of the grey lake and the other children, he looked at the picture, because he never got tired of it.

It was a picture of the Lord Jesus sitting in a field of flowers, and the children of the world all around him, looking up into his face. On the grass at his feet sat a black boy, and at his knee was an Indian child. His arms were thrown round a little girl in a blue dress, and the children of China and the South Seas were nestling up to him.

It was about a week after the operation when Dani and Annette first talked properly about that picture. It had been a still, grey day, with dull clouds lying low over the lake. Twilight had fallen early. The lights were on, and most of the children were asleep, but Annette still sat beside Dani. She had stayed late the past few days because he was so restless without her.

Now he lay with his arms flung above his head on his pillow, his fair hair pushed back from his hot forehead and his blue eyes very bright. He was tired, tired, tired, and wanted to go to sleep so badly. But the pain in his leg kept him awake. So he rolled his head round to look at the picture with the writing underneath.

"What does it say, Nette?" asked Dani suddenly.

"It says, 'Let the children come to me'," replied Annette, who was looking, too.

"I know that story," went on the weary little voice; "Grandma told it to me. Are those the children in the Bible?"

"No," said Annette, "they aren't the children in the Bible. They are other children from all over the world – Indians and Africans, and the little girl is probably Swiss. All the children are wearing their national costumes, I think… the costumes of their countries."

"Why?" asked Dani.

"Well, I suppose to show that all children can come to Jesus, not just the ones in the Bible."

"How?" asked Dani.

"Well, I don't quite know how to explain. You just say you want to come, Dani, and then you're there. I suppose Jesus sort of picks you up in his arms, like the children in the Bible, even though you can't see him."

"Oh," said Dani, "I see. Annette, my leg hurts so badly. I wish I could go to sleep."

He began to cry fretfully and throw his arms about. Annette shook up his pillows, gave him a drink, and he sank back with a tired sigh.

"Sing to me," he commanded, and Annette sang very softly because she was shy of the nurse hearing.

Oh! que Ta main paternelle
Me bénisse à mon coucher!

And as she sang, Dani closed his eyes.

But in the few seconds that passed when he was not quite awake or quite asleep, Dani thought he saw the picture again. But the girl in the blue dress had gone, and in her place, with Jesus' arms about him, was a thin little boy with rumpled, sun-bleached hair. And on the grass at his feet lay a pair of crutches with bears' heads carved on them.

"It's me," said Dani to himself, and fell fast asleep for sheer joy.

Several things happened while Dani lay sleeping. Firstly, Monsieur Givet came and lifted one of the weights off his leg. Secondly, his fever left him. Thirdly, a warm south wind came breathing over the land, scattering the clouds and clearing the sky.

Dani slept and slept and slept, and when he woke up he thought he must somehow have got into a new world. He lay quite still thinking about it for a long time. He felt cool and comfortable, and his leg had stopped hurting. The big glass doors of the ward had been flung open. Through them Dani could see, for the first time, sparkling blue water, misty blue mountains on the other side of the lake, and a blue sky swept clean by the south winds. Tiny ragged white clouds strayed all over it – baby clouds, skipping about. They reminded Dani of baby goats skipping about in fields where the snow had melted and the crocuses had sprung up.

"I'm going to get well," said Dani to himself, taking long breaths of sweet, cool air. The breeze through the door smelt of wet earth and warm rain. He shut his eyes and suddenly knew with a great surge of joy that spring was coming. And as he lay sniffing and listening, one bird began to sing. It sang with all its might, as though it were the sole herald of the great awakening.

"It's coming, coming, coming!" shouted the bird. "You're going to get well, well, well!"

The door opened, and Annette clattered up the ward, warm and rosy from the wind. She usually popped across after breakfast just to see how he was.

"Isn't it a lovely day, Dani?" she cried. "Look at the lake and the mountains on the other side, and the little ships."

Dani turned his head solemnly towards her.

"Annette, where are my bear crutches?"

"Here, Dani, behind your locker. Why?"

"Well, you know that poor little boy in the corner? He might like them. Give them to him."

"But why, Dani? You like them so much yourself."

"I know. But I shan't want them any more. I'm going to get better and run about in ordinary boots."

And he was quite right. He never did want them any more. He got perfectly well.

26

Just as the weeks passed in the valley, so the weeks passed in the mountains, and the snows began to melt and the little streams became torrents, and the first crocuses pushed up in the fields along the river. The cattle and goats shut up in the stables began to stamp restlessly and cry for freedom. South winds came sweeping up the valleys and the sap in the pine trees rose and smelt sweet in the forests. Spring was coming to the mountains.

Grandmother was busy with the spring-cleaning and Father was busy with the new calves. This was a good thing, for when they were busy they did not miss the children quite so badly, although every new pink-nosed calf reminded Father of Dani. Grandmother was really much too old and blind to be spring-cleaning. She would often sit down suddenly beside the half scrubbed furniture. Then, half awake and half dreaming, she would imagine she heard the hop and clatter of one boot and crutches climbing the steps, and the happy sound of a little boy singing. But she would wake to the sad silence and wonder for the 1,000th time how much longer it would be before they came home.

Lucien missed them, too. He never walked home alone without wishing Annette was walking beside him. But he was not lonely or unhappy at school any longer. He had proved to them that he was sorry by his dangerous journey across the mountain and the children had accepted him back as one of themselves.

And Lucien himself was different. Ever since the Saviour had come into his heart he had known that there must be a difference. The old bad temper and laziness and unhappiness could not stay for long in a heart that was open to the love of Jesus. And gradually Lucien began to find that, as long as he kept close to the Lord by praying and reading his Bible every day, the love was stronger than the bad temper and the laziness. He knew that he was growing into a new sort of boy who could keep his temper when teased, and who didn't mind doing the nasty jobs.

Often when school was over he would go across to Grandmother's house and help with the spring-cleaning. They were great friends. Indeed, Grandmother would hardly have known what to do without him, for he chopped her wood and did her shopping. He also brought any letters up from the village, and this he liked doing best of all for they were usually from Annette. Grandmother always got him to read them aloud to her. There was sometimes a picture from Dani, too. Grandmother kept them all safely in the front of her Bible and often spread them out on the table to look at them. By the end of February she had a collection of pictures entitled 'Me in bed', 'Me not in bed', 'Me chasing goats', 'Me having medicine', 'Me and nurse', 'Me and Annette', 'Me and Snowball the kitten'. Grandmother thought the pictures were very good, although in the last one she and Lucien had had some difficulty making out which was 'Me' and which was 'Snowball the kitten'.

But a sadness came into Lucien's life just then. His friend, the old woodcarver, was to leave the mountain and go down to the lake to live with his son, Monsieur Givet. It had all been arranged that afternoon when they first recognised each other.

He was to leave at the beginning of March. The day before he left, Lucien climbed up through the forest to help him pack. He had farmed out the goat and the cat and the hens, and sold nearly all his little figures. But he was not selling the house. He was just shutting it up till he came back.

"I shall often come back, Lucien," he explained. "I couldn't leave the mountain for long. I'll stop down there for a while, but then I shall hear the mountains calling me, and back I'll come for a bit of a holiday."

He looked thoughtfully across the valley, and then glanced round the bare shelves of the hut.

"I'm taking a few of my figures for the children," he remarked. "They may like them. And one, Lucien, I kept for you. I came across it when I was going through them the other night. It's one I thought I couldn't part with, but I'd like you to have it if you'd care for it."

Lucien looked up eagerly.

"I'd love to have one, Monsieur," he replied. "It will remind me of you. And, besides, I might be able to copy it."

The old man went to the cupboard and drew out the gift he had laid aside for Lucien. He put it in the boy's hands and watched him closely as he examined it.

It looked simple enough at first sight. It was a wooden cross made of two pieces of rough wood, but the cross-beam was bound to the post by exquisitely carved ropes twisted in knots, a filigree work of fine wood. Lucien's fingers touched the perfect craftsmanship reverently, and he lifted shining eyes to his old master.

"It's beautiful," he cried. "I can't think how you carved those ropes without breaking the wood." And then he added, very shyly, "It's the cross where Jesus was crucified, isn't it?"

"Yes," replied the old man simply. "I carved it the night my old master died... the night he spoke to me about the love and mercy of God, and the night I believed I could be forgiven. Once, you and I had a talk about loving. The cross is the place where we see love made perfect."

Lucien looked up again quickly.

"Perfect love!" he repeated. "I am always hearing about that these days! It's what Annette and I talked about the night before she went away."

"Yes," agreed the old man. "You'll often hear it! Perfect love… it means love that goes on doing until there isn't anything more to be done. Love that goes on suffering till it can't suffer any more. That's why, when Jesus hung on the cross, he said, 'Everything is done!' There wasn't one bad thing left that couldn't be forgiven, not one person who had done wrong who couldn't be saved, because he had died. He had loved perfectly."

The old man seemed to have forgotten Lucien and to be talking to himself. But Lucien was listening all the same. He said goodbye to the old man, and promised to come up early next morning and carry his pack to the station on the way to school. Then he ran home through the spring twilight, to the sound of the snow dripping from the branches as the warm wind stirred through them. He was in a hurry because he wanted to write to Annette so that the old man could take the letter with him next morning. But the first thing to do was to hang his little cross carefully above his bed. Then he ran to the kitchen to find a pen and paper.

The kitchen was in rather a mess. His mother was over with the cows and had not had time to wash the pans or empty the bucket. Lucien usually helped her, but tonight he was in a hurry. If he slipped back into his bedroom he could write undisturbed, and she would clear the mess and not know he had come in.

He hurried off and curled himself up on the floor by his bed. He was just starting when he happened to glance up and caught sight of the carved cross hanging on the wall.

He stared at it for a moment or two, thinking hard. What was it the old man had said? "Perfect love" – strange he should hear those words again – "Perfect love … goes on doing until there isn't anything more to be done."

He, in some tiny measure, wanted to be like the Saviour and to love perfectly, too. And there were all those dirty pans out in the kitchen waiting to be washed.

He went rather red and got up slowly. When his mother came in half an hour later she found the kitchen looking clean and tidy and a happy-hearted Lucien sitting writing at the table.

He went up to the old man early next morning while the forest was still dark, and they came down together, leaving the lonely chalet to wait for his return. As they reached the margin of the trees the mists broke in the valley, the cocks crew, and the sun touched the high peaks.

The old man boarded the train that had carried away Annette and Dani, with his eyes fixed wistfully on the mountains.

"When the narcissi begin to come out, I shall come back," he reminded Lucien, as the train was starting off. "You write and tell me when they're out in the valley. That will give me plenty of time to get back, before they flower on the mountain. Don't forget, Lucien."

But Lucien's reply was drowned by the clatter of milk churns as the train jolted off and disappeared round the bend of the hill.

It was not very long after this that Lucien collected a letter for Grandmother from the post office. He hurried up the hill to give it to her, for he knew it was from Annette.

He clattered up the veranda steps shouting the good news, and Grandmother came eagerly out.

"Read it to me, Lucien," she said. And she sat down in the sunshine, folding her hands and shutting her eyes so as to listen without distraction.

It was a very short letter, and Lucien read it all in a breath.

"Dear Father and Grandmother," it ran. "Dani and I are coming home the day after tomorrow. Dani is quite well again. We are longing to see you, and Dani says please bring Klaus to the station. Your loving Annette."

There was also a note from Madame Givet giving the exact time of their arrival, and a masterpiece from Dani entitled 'Me coming home on the train'.

Just for a few minutes Grandmother began to cry, the shaky little cry of a very weak old woman. But she quickly wiped away her tears and pretended to become a very strong old woman, because there was such a lot to be done.

"Go over to the shed and give that letter to Monsieur Burnier, Lucien," she said firmly, "and then come back here and help me right away. There's a lot to be done. There are beds to be aired, cakes to be cooked and the furniture to be polished. We must have everything looking its best for the children."

Father, on receiving the news, said, "Oh – er!" and scratched his head. Then for the first time in his life he upset the milk pail, and shortly afterwards disappeared into the forest and didn't come back for a long time.

The next day dawned clear and beautiful. There was no school. Lucien was up at daybreak picking primulas and crocuses and snowdrops and soldanellas. He arranged them in a bowl on the veranda table and then set out for the station, walking slowly because there was plenty of time and plenty to think about. Grandmother, Father, and Klaus (wearing a new pink bow) had gone in the mule cart.

Surely there had never been such a spring morning! The fields where the grass had been yellow and crushed were unbelievably green and starred with flowers. The air was full of the bells of cattle newly released from their winter prison and drunk with spring and liberty. Baby goats gambolled in the meadows, and thrushes shouted from the orchards. The forests were heavy with the scent of sap, and the white peaks pierced a sky so blue that it dazzled the eyes to look at it.

It's not unlike the day, almost a year ago, when Dani fell, thought Lucien. A clump of crocuses reminded him of it. What a dark day that had been. The very remembrance of it shadowed his happy thoughts. It had all been his fault that Annette and Dani had ever had to go away. Perhaps after all they wouldn't be so very pleased to see him. Annette had said Dani was well, but Lucien could hardly believe it.

He reached the station in a rather nervous state of mind. He stood apart with his hands in his pockets, because he suddenly felt a little afraid of meeting them, and wished he hadn't come. A lot of people were there so the tiny platform was quite crowded. Father kept his eyes fixed on the far point down the valley where the train would appear between the mountains. Grandmother struggled with Klaus, who seemed to wish to set off down the line and meet the train on her own.

"It's coming!" said Father. Everyone crowded forward, except for Lucien who was feeling shyer than ever.

And now it had come, and Annette and Dani were at the window, rosy with excitement and clamouring to be let out.

Dani gave one glance at the group of well-loved faces all pressed so close to welcome him, and in that glance he noticed Lucien standing apart. For an instant he wondered why. His loving, happy little heart wanted to gather together all the people he knew and loved. He tumbled out of the train, broke through the crowd, and ran straight to Lucien.

"Look, Lucien," he shouted. "I can walk! Your doctor you found made me better, and I can run just as though I never fell. Look, Grandma! Look, Papa! I'm running without my crutches! And look, Klaus, here's your kitten. Isn't he big, Grandma? Nearly as big as Klaus!"

Klaus and the kitten simply hated each other, and snarled and scratched and hissed. Dani and Grandmother struggled to keep them apart, the crowd laughed, the train rattled off, and Annette clung to her father as though she would never let go of him again.

Only Lucien had turned away, because he found there were tears in his eyes. He had been honoured above everybody. His great wrong was forgiven and forgotten for ever. Dani could walk just as though he had never fallen.

And as he turned he noticed that the almond tree on the platform had burst into flower at the top. Yesterday there was nothing but bare branches. But spring had proved too strong for it, and straight from the naked wood had crowded the starry pink blossoms.

The winter was over and gone, the flowers had appeared on the earth. The time of the singing of birds had come.

Star of Light

When Hamid finds out that his little blind sister is to be sold to a beggar, he runs away with her from their mountain village to a town. But, in the town, they are alone and there doesn't seem to be any way to find a new home. Then they hear of a nurse who works with street children and Hamid does something desparate to help his sister.

ISBN 978 1 84427 296 9
Price £4.99

The Mystery of Pheasant Cottage

Lucy has lived with her grandparents at Pheasant Cottage but she has dim memories of someone else. Who was it? What are her grandparents hiding from her? Lucy is makes her mind up to find the answers, but it turns out to be harder than she expected.

ISBN 978 1 84427 297 6
Price £4.99

These books are available from your local Christian bookshop, SU Mail Order (0845 07 06 006) or at www.scriptureunion.org.uk/shop